AMISH INN MYSTERIES™

A Silent Betrayal

Rachael O. Phillips

Annie's®

AnniesFiction.com

Library of Congress-in-Publication Data
A Silent Betrayal/ by Rachael O. Phillips
p. cm.
I. Title
                    2016955034

AnniesFiction.com
(800) 282-6643
Amish Inn Mysteries™
Series Creator: Shari Lohner
Series Editors: Lorie Jones and Shari Lohner
Cover Illustrator: Kelley McMorris

10 11 12 13 14 | Printed in China | 9 8 7 6 5 4 3 2

1

Liz Eckardt savored the Indian summer day outside her Olde Mansion Inn, listening as the breeze rustled through scarlet, gold, and russet leaves, confiding its secrets.

But the wind should have saved its breath.

Sadie Schwarzentruber's big, pink motorcycle blasted away the serenity that normally prevailed on an afternoon in Pleasant Creek, Indiana. She and her raucous steed roared once around the town square, with its tall clock tower, then started another lap.

Mary Ann Berne, Sadie's friend and business partner, pressed a perfectly manicured hand to her forehead. "Sadie has been riding that thing every day. Sometimes three or four times. Maybe I can talk the police into arresting her."

"You wouldn't do that," Liz said, though she wasn't sure she meant it.

Mary Ann sighed. "I guess Chief Houghton wouldn't arrest her anyway."

Liz grinned. "You have clout with the chief but not that much. I think he likes Sadie's motorcycle almost as much as she does."

"If only she'd run a stoplight or something and have to pay a hefty fine."

Fat chance. Though the local police tolerated Sadie's self-designed traffic rules when driving her business van, they would have cracked down on her when riding her "hog." Sadie knew the unofficial official stance: Set a good example for our teens on that motorcycle, and we'll look away when you're double-parked.

Three local Amish women, including Liz's cousin Miriam Borkholder, rode up on bicycles, slowing to a stop. They'd come, Liz surmised, to shop in Mary Ann and Sadie's sewing store, Sew Welcome, housed in Liz's bed-and-breakfast.

Miriam hopped nimbly from her seat and gave Liz the quick side hug the Amish permitted in public for kinfolk. Motioning at her companions, she said, "You know Rose and Mattie Stoltzfus, don't you, Liz?"

Mary Ann, acquainted with the family trees of everyone in Pleasant Creek, obviously knew them already.

"I believe we've met." Liz smiled at the young women, trying to recall the barn raising or town event where she'd seen them. With heart-shaped, pink-cheeked faces, large blue eyes, and corn-colored hair, the sisters resembled so many other pretty Amish girls.

Rose answered with a small smile and a barely audible greeting.

Mattie, who appeared several years younger than her sister, said, "I saw you at the Christmas parade last year with the mayor."

Liz's cheeks warmed. Most girls, Amish and English, noticed Jackson Cross's rugged good looks.

"I'm trying to persuade these two to bike with me in the festival's Kappel Apple Ride, but they haven't agreed yet." Miriam and her family, like everyone else in the area, were preparing for the Harvest Festival, a multitown celebration spanning more than a week that attracted huge crowds to their quiet county every fall.

Mattie's eyes sparked, and Rose shook her head. "Perhaps someday. This year, we might help at the food and water stops."

The note of longing in her "someday" caught Liz's ear. Though the local bishop no doubt forbade his flock to participate in the Kappel Apple Race, he apparently allowed them to join the noncompetitive ride. What was holding them back?

Her musings ended as Sadie and her motorcycle rounded a corner and rocketed toward them. The sisters raised their heads like deer in a pasture. Liz would have dived for cover had she not known Sadie possessed incredible coordination.

Instead, Liz merely winced as Sadie stopped a few inches from the sidewalk. The motorcycle exhaled a grumbling, rumbling protest before quiet reigned.

If Sadie's drama had startled Rose and Mattie, her getup widened their eyes until they seemed to fill the girls' faces. Miriam kept her usual calm, but a grin threatened to escape her controlled demeanor.

Liz didn't bother to hide her smile, tinged with envy. Sadie ate anything and everything she liked. Yet her lean, wiry figure, whittled by heavy farmwork, could rival that of a rider forty years younger. Lines of metal studs adorned her formfitting outfit. *It's simply not fair that a woman over seventy should look that awesome in black leather.*

Sadie yanked off her silver and magenta helmet. "Pink Penelope's in great form today. Wish I could really turn her loose on the highway. It's just wrong that she can't race the way she wants to."

Mary Ann snorted. "The way *she* wants to? That thing is only a machine. You're the one who wants to break the sound barrier."

"That would be exciting," Sadie said wistfully.

"Stick to your tractor." Mary Ann interposed her own slim frame between the motorcycle and the aghast Amish sisters. "Please go on inside, ladies. The shop's door is unlocked. Feel free to look around, and I'll follow in a minute or two."

Miriam, who wore the black *Kapp* of a married woman, gave a slight wink and steered Rose and Mattie toward the inn's front door.

Mary Ann shook her head at Sadie. Liz could tell her no-nonsense friend was trying to corral a smile, but it broke through. "Okay, you've had your fun, Sadie. We still have tons to do before the Harvest Festival. Go park that thing and change."

Sadie thumbed her nose at Mary Ann. "Not unless I can have pie."

"Of course we'll have pie. I brought coconut cream, remember? And Dutch apple and cherry."

Sadie guided a somewhat subdued Penelope to the inn's parking lot.

"Sadie may putt around on that motorcycle for a little while, but I imagine she'll show up for work." Liz grinned. Coconut cream was Sadie's favorite.

Mary Ann returned the grin. "You come and have pie too."

Now it was Liz's turn to be wistful. Mary Ann's pies were famous, even among the Amish. "I'd love to, but I'm expecting guests any minute now."

"What, it's illegal for them to see you eat pie? Well, never mind. I'll bring the pies to coffee hour."

"Oh, thanks." While the freshly baked cookies that Liz normally provided for her guests during the inn's afternoon coffee hour would have spelled hospitality, Mary Ann's pies would make them want to stay forever.

"Are your guests coming for the festival?" Mary Ann cocked her head. "It's only Wednesday. Why so early?"

Liz shrugged. "They said something about setting up booths."

Sudden thunder growled, then boomed as not one, but a dozen motorcycles passed Liz.

Mary Ann rolled her eyes and hurried inside.

Well, what can we expect with the festival's Hog Wild Ride? Soon the whole county would vibrate with the rumble of motorcycles, spooking people and animals alike. How would the Amish, who depended on their horses, manage during the coming week? The Hog Wild Ride, appropriately held in nearby Wildton, had been part of the festival for decades. So perhaps the horses had learned to tolerate the racket.

Liz turned to admire the effect of her inn's red siding and white trim against the colorful fall foliage. When she'd left her job as a corporate patent attorney in Boston and moved to Indiana, she'd had no idea that a Midwestern autumn could be so lovely. Or that this small, quaint town could win her heart in such a short time. Finding her late mother's Amish family, including Miriam, had warmed Liz's lonely world. Miriam was like the sister she'd never had.

And the Material Girls—the quilting group that met at Sew Welcome, including Mary Ann and Sadie—not only sewed together; they also laughed, played, and occasionally argued. But they always had each other's backs during tough times.

Three huge, deafening motorcycles veered off Main Street into the inn's parking lot, interrupting Liz's reverie. Six of Liz's eleven guests had arrived for a two-day setup for the festival, which began Friday evening. One rider approached Sadie, who still lingered by her bike. Soon most of the group had gathered around her, patting Pink Penelope with admiration in their voices.

Liz waited a few moments before she approached the group of tired-looking riders and extended her hand. Their leader wasn't hard to pick out; he towered over everyone.

The man hesitated, and then his enormous paw shook Liz's. His deep voice rumbled through his black beard, reminding her of his bike's sound. "This is the Olde Mansion Inn, isn't it?"

"You're in the right place." Liz smiled.

"You certainly are, Big Berky." Sadie gestured toward the house. "By the end of the festival, Liz will have you so spoiled, you won't want to go home."

"Spoiled. That sounds nice," drawled a tall, sinuous young woman wearing clothing embellished with skulls and lace. She shot the big man a playful yet pointed look. "Not like the last place we stayed."

"We're here, okay?" Like a giant tortoise, Big Berky seemed to pull in his head. He knelt beside his motorcycle and began to tinker.

The woman turned to Liz. "I'm Honey Wilson. I made our reservations." The color of her long, thick ponytail matched her name.

"I remember. So glad to meet you, Honey. Your three rooms are ready whenever you want them. We have coffee hour around four, with complimentary refreshments. Usually we serve cookies, but my friend Mary Ann is bringing her incredible pies too."

Big Berky glanced up from his bike. A flash of interest awakened in his bearded face. "At four?"

Laughing, Honey knelt, threw her arms around his bull neck, and kissed him. "You can handle that, right?"

"I get first dibs on the coconut cream," Sadie declared.

The other two women bikers chuckled.

Big Berky stood and pointed. "All right if we chain the bikes to these things?"

"They're hitching posts," Liz said. "For horses."

"Horses?" His face wrinkled. "Oh yeah. You have lots of them around here."

"All the businesses in Pleasant Creek have hitching posts for Amish customers," Liz explained. "But they'll work for motorcycles as well. Please feel free."

She waved and turned back toward the inn. These would be the first bandanna-wearing guests she'd entertained, but in some ways, people were all the same—at least when it came to Mary Ann's pies.

Soon afterward, the bikers registered. Honey, whose given name was Carissa, introduced the whole group, explaining that Robert, Mary Katherine, George, and Tiffany also preferred to be addressed by their biker names: Scooby, Pixie, Bulldog, and Shine.

Big Berky, Honey informed Liz, received his nickname at birth. He was the biggest baby ever born in their hometown of Berkville, Kentucky.

Her boyfriend tolerated that, but he growled when she told Liz his real name—Sherwood.

No wonder he preferred his biker handle.

"Bulldog, meet our own bulldog." Liz grinned as she introduced her guest to Beans, the über-relaxed, brown-and-white canine Liz had inherited when she purchased the inn.

When Bulldog scratched the dog's ears, Beans wagged his stubby tail for two seconds, an astonishingly energetic display of approval.

Watching them, Liz realized the biker had chosen an appropriate nickname. Though good-looking in his own way, Bulldog resembled Beans, with his stocky build, broad face, and slightly pushed-in nose.

The encounter appeared to have drained Beans's tiny reservoir of energy. He plopped onto his favorite rug—Liz's too, unfortunately—near the front door of the foyer. Bulldog gave him a final pat and headed upstairs to his room.

Soon, two more young men carrying bicycle helmets and large duffel bags approached Liz's rotunda desk.

The shorter, clean-shaven blond guy plunked his luggage in front of the desk and introduced himself as Jason Brummett. He and his friend Trent Cleveland had come to ride the Harvest Festival's Kappel Apple Race on Saturday, a hundred-mile bicycle competition that attracted cyclists from several states.

Tall, dark Trent was drop-dead gorgeous. His lightning once-over of the inn rubbed Liz the wrong way. Like her ex-boyfriend Matt, he seemed to pose for photo ops even without a camera present.

Trent said, "I'm really allergic to peanuts. So don't have them around, okay?"

Notice beforehand would have been nice. Forcing a smile, Liz said, "I'll remove them immediately from the kitchen and the inn's common areas, like the sitting and dining rooms. But I can't guarantee you won't come into contact with peanut residue or that other guests won't have peanuts in their rooms."

Trent sighed. "We'll have to go somewhere else."

"Are you kidding, man? There isn't any other place to stay," Jason objected. "Besides, this lady wants to work with you as much as other hotels have. Do you want to race or not?"

Trent swore, but he shrugged and said, "Whatever."

Jason's nice-boy smile cooled Liz's hot annoyance somewhat. She arranged for their bicycles to be housed in the inn's garage and gave them keys to the Somewhere in Time Room, which featured antique clocks.

As the cyclists hauled their bags upstairs, she reviewed all the room assignments: Scooby and Bulldog had taken the Amish Room, with its plain but cheerful decor; Honey and Shine, despite their skull-themed attire, had oohed and aahed over the frilly Rose of Sharon Room. Big Berky had received the Sunrise Room because his snores reached jet-plane noise levels. The simple, colorful Sunset Room suited Pixie, who preferred solitude. That left the spacious Heirloom Room, which Liz sometimes decorated as a bridal suite, for the three women yet to arrive.

She'd added little autumn touches here and there in the rooms. But she missed the floral artistry of Kiera Williams, her teenage gardener, who was so busy with finishing high school and taking junior college courses that she'd had to quit until next summer.

Satisfaction eased Liz's pang in missing blunt, capable Kiera herself. The girl had come a long way since she'd more or less bullied Liz into giving her a job.

Liz pushed her thoughts back to business. Would her last three guests be cyclists? Bikers? Or perhaps they were planning to explore the festival and shop until they dropped?

A full inn was a bed-and-breakfast owner's dream, but it could become a nightmare without thorough preparation. She'd better fold more towels.

Liz hurried to the utility room and dumped a huge load of fluffy towels from the big commercial dryer into a basket. As she whipped through the pile, she vacillated between hoping for older, quieter guests and younger ones whose hours, energy, and interests would mesh better with the present ones.

Liz often played a private game in which she imagined her own version of her next guest. Sometimes she hit the bull's-eye. Occasionally, she missed the target. With visitors from all kinds of backgrounds parking their suitcases in her B&B, she was never bored. Kandace Somebody had booked the reservations. Liz made herself a mental bet that Kandace would be young because her name began with a nontraditional K. If she went by Kandy, she definitely would be young. And blonde. Brushing back her own blonde hair from her face, Liz grinned at the irony of her hunch. She'd shrugged off the "dumb blonde" label forever ago in junior high.

A bang from the screen door and a "Hey!" told her forty-something Naomi Mason, the other Material Girl her own age, must have closed her bakery early. She hoped her hardworking friend would get a break before Harvest Festival demands kept her busy day and night. Liz called, "I'm in the utility room."

"I could have guessed that." Naomi entered and grabbed several folded towels from the swaying stack in Liz's arms. "Want me to help with delivery duty? Or anything else?"

"You'll be running yourself ragged soon enough."

But Naomi headed toward the rotunda stairway.

Liz snagged a tin bucket of handmade soaps and followed, glad to spend a few minutes with her friend any way she could. "Thanks to Sarah, the rooms are ready." Sarah Borkholder, Liz's Amish maid, always cleaned the inn as if she herself were expecting company. "I've stuffed the pantry, and the freezer's full of cookies and breads for coffee hour."

"You know that in the event of an emergency sugar shortage, you can always raid my place." Naomi's dark eyes twinkled as she clambered up the stairs.

"You have no idea what that means to me. In fact, if I had a brain and more money, I wouldn't even touch an oven." Liz halted on the landing, loving the antique sconces and mirrors that reflected her autumn arrangement of sunflowers, wheat stalks, and small pumpkins on a long, narrow table. She pointed toward the linen closet. "If you'll put the towels in there, I'll take these to—"

Footsteps bumped and clunked from the stairs above. Big Berky, torn Harley-Davidson T-shirt barely covering his broad shoulders and beer belly, lumbered down. He paused, apparently to ask Liz a question.

At the same time, Trent Cleveland, wearing sleek, professional cyclist's garb and a photo-ready smile, emerged from his room. The smile thinned.

The two men exchanged only one glance.

But what a glance.

Gorilla, said Trent's.

Spandex boy, said Berky's.

Liz crossed their line of vision and pretended to consult Naomi about something. To Liz's relief, Big Berky continued down the stairs. Trent appraised Naomi's curves, then asked, to Liz's surprise, if his girlfriend and her two friends could keep their bikes in the garage too.

"I may need that space for our other guests," Liz hedged.

"But Kandy will be staying here. And Jessi and Stephanie. They're riding the women's race on Saturday too."

So Kandy must be Kandace. *Poor girl.* "Certainly. I'll mention it to her when she checks in."

"She just texted me that she's downstairs."

Naomi stacked her towels on the table and took Liz's load. "Where do you want these?"

Liz told her and rushed down to the rotunda where a twenty-something with a long, blonde French braid down her back waited. *Bull's-eye!*

"About time you got here, Kandy." Trent brushed past Liz, lines furrowing his forehead.

Where's your smile, Casanova? With difficulty, Liz kept her own in place.

"We hit traffic in Indianapolis." His girlfriend turned to Liz. "I'm Kandace Forbes. Stephanie Galt and Jessi Hanover are outside with our bikes—"

"You can store them in the garage. Already took care of that." Trent grabbed her bag. "I'm starving. Get your key, and let's find someplace to eat."

"If you'd like, come for complimentary coffee hour in a few minutes," Liz offered. "My friend Mary Ann brought her famous pies."

"That sounds really good." Kandy's tired face brightened.

Liz almost hoped she'd cave to Trent's pressure—would he demand a whole pie for himself? But her boyfriend decided that sounded okay. If it was ready in a few minutes.

After Liz handed Kandy the room keys, the cyclist left her duffel bag with Liz. She and Trent exited to help the others store the bikes.

"Wow, that guy is a real piece of work." Naomi descended, frowning at the closed door.

"You're telling me." Liz picked up the duffel bag. "Maybe he'll be more likable after he's had something to eat. I've never met a disposition yet that didn't improve after eating Mary Ann's pie."

"That would be a first," Naomi agreed. She sighed. "Wish I could stay, but I need to clean the bakery from top to bottom. I sure won't have time to do it after the festival starts. Plus, I'd like to go to bed early."

"Good idea." Liz knew her friend would get up at three thirty or earlier to make sure Sweet Everything was stocked with her very best pastries.

Naomi waved, then paused at the front door. "Want me to pray for your coffee hour?"

"Prayers would be welcome. Especially if both Trent and Big Berky come."

Naomi shook her head as she left. "Have fun."

Oh yeah. Liz hurried to the beverage bar and replenished her supply of coffee. *If those two—and their riding buddies—don't get along, the fun is just beginning.*

2

Liz loved it when she was right. Especially this time.

With a slice from each of Mary Ann's pies, Trent had cheered up considerably.

So had all the cycling and biker guests who had arrived to drink coffee around the fireplace in the sitting room.

Except Kandy. Her blue eyes blanked to gray as her temperamental Prince Charming seemed determined to woo every woman in the inn. Trent's smooth, effortless charisma reached like tentacles toward anything female.

Liz winced inwardly as she carried used plates and cups to the kitchen. Even clock-conscious Mary Ann, who had to leave early for a final Harvest Festival committee meeting, had stayed longer than she'd planned. Sadie, still wearing black leather, preened as she followed every word Trent said.

At the moment, the cyclist was talking about his daily regimen and his expert take on supplements. "I've developed a special combination of vitamins that have helped build my endurance so that it peaks at exactly the right time. Instead of dying near the end of a race, I can sprint for the finish." Though he aimed a barbed look at his girlfriend, he said silkily, "It might work for you if only you'd try it."

Kandy ignored him, but Liz noticed her slender fingers curled into a fist.

Actually, aren't you more into pie power, Trent? Liz wished she could make the snarky remark aloud. The guy was so full of himself—way too much like Matt.

"Vitamins." Big Berky crossed his muscled arms. "Take a bunch of pills to ride a bicycle like a kid? No way. Now my Harley—that's a real bike."

"No, it's not a real bike, even if you call yourself a biker. As a cyclist, I supply my own power." Trent's gaze lingered on the biker's paunch. "And the vitamins? They help me win. A lot. Not to mention, I stay in top shape."

"Let's ride together sometime soon," Berky sneered. "I'll leave you and your kiddie bicycle in the dust."

Liz intervened, offering more pie, and the two retreated to separate corners.

Still, Trent managed to drive the conversation toward himself. He talked about winning a contest run by Gulp! The prominent sports-drink manufacturer now sponsored him, making it possible for Trent to quit his day job. Training full-time, he was certain he would rise to national prominence.

Honey leaned toward Trent. She couldn't take her smoky, hazel eyes from his handsome face.

By now, Big Berky looked even less cheerful than Kandy. He'd hardly sampled his second piece of pie, a sure sign of trouble. The other men—Jason, Bulldog, and Scooby—said little and mostly concentrated on eating.

Liz was racking her brain for something that would break Trent's spell when the cavalry arrived from an unlikely source.

Beans.

True to usual habit, he had slept on his rug all afternoon. But now Beans approached Bulldog as if they were long-lost relatives. Tail wagging furiously, the dog nosed the man's knee, then licked it, bulgy eyes alight.

"Hey, boy, you want more?" Bulldog reached into his pocket. "I gave him something earlier," he explained to Liz, who was busily refilling carafes.

"Now he'll be your friend forever," she warned with a smile as she left to fetch more cream and sugar. Hearing laughter as she returned, Liz thanked heaven for Beans's comic relief.

His face wore a wide doggy smile, but he chewed and chewed like a kid with a mouthful of bubble gum.

Bulldog patted the dog's bobbing head. "Peanut butter can do that to you, right, Beans?"

Liz choked.

"Peanut butter?" Trent shot to his feet.

"Um, yeah." Bulldog frowned. "Chill, man. It's a sandwich. Not poison or something."

"For me, it is." Trent backed away to the far end of the room. "I'm violently allergic to peanuts. Get that dog out of here."

Liz seized Beans's collar and tried to lead him out of the room, but convinced that Bulldog possessed an infinite supply of peanut butter in his pockets, the animal dropped his big rump like an anchor.

"Come on, Beans. Sweet doggy, you need a nap, don't you? Poor Beans, this is too much for you. Let's go lie down now . . ." Only with the help of Sadie's wiry strength and baby-talk urgings did Beans finally return to his rug.

Gritting her teeth, Liz dashed back to the sitting room. Could she salvage coffee hour?

From the expressions on Trent's and Big Berky's faces, that looked like mission impossible.

"Allergic to peanut butter?" The burly biker eyed Trent as if he were a slug. "Well, it figures."

Glowering, Trent crossed his arms. "What exactly do you mean by that?"

Honey jumped up and glared at Berky. "What is the matter with you? Making fun of somebody with a medical condition!"

"I'm sure no one here wants to upset anyone." Liz blended a soothing mother tone with her Lawyer Liz persona. "Now that everyone knows about Trent's allergy, I suggest we all try hard to avoid another difficult situation."

Red-faced Bulldog nodded.

Still wearing his injured air, Trent grunted.

Big Berky muttered something under his breath, but having received an elbow from Honey, he nodded too.

Bulldog stood and mumbled, "Sorry, Trent. Didn't mean to cause trouble." He left, followed by most of the group. All except Trent and Kandy. And Honey.

Kandy tugged on Trent's arm. "C'mon. Let's go for a ride."

He didn't budge. "Don't feel like it. Maybe later."

"The sun sets earlier here." She stood. "I need a ride now."

"Well, go if you want."

Aiming a backward look like an arrow, Kandy left.

Liz lingered, picking up stray silverware, wiping invisible crumbs from end tables. She wished she dared drag out her big vacuum. She'd used that ploy when her godson, Steve, whom she had raised, stayed in his room too long with a date.

But Trent and Honey weren't teens.

From the locked look between them, not even a street sweeper charging through the room would interrupt their fascinating conversation.

———— /////////////////////// ————

"Great breakfast." Jason rubbed his stomach appreciatively as he waited for Trent and Kandy in the foyer. "Plenty of carbs and protein with no grease. We've got lots to do today, so it hit the spot."

"Thanks." Liz, working on finances on her laptop, had found the recipe for the egg and turkey sausage casserole on an athletes' website.

She paused as Jason explained that he, Trent, and the women cyclists had reserved today to help the bicycling association set up the SAG—Support and Gear—tent. They'd also organize supplies for the men's and women's Kappel Apple Races and the noncompetitive Kappel Apple Ride on Saturday. Plus, they'd check out the routes, noting special challenges like confusing markings, blind turns, and busy intersections.

Other members of their cycling club would arrive tomorrow, staying in nearby hotels and B&Bs.

Jason told Liz they'd probably work all day and grab supper somewhere. "Guess the bikers are doing the same thing. Scooby told me yesterday that twenty-five riders from their group are coming tomorrow too."

After yesterday's coffee hour fiasco, a pleasant chat with Jason this morning lifted Liz's spirits.

Stephanie and Jessi appeared, helmets in hand, looking ready to roll. Liz enjoyed exchanging pleasantries.

Trent and Kandy descended the stairs, seemingly absorbed in their plans for the day. He even appeared to listen to her.

A civilized conversation? *Yes.* Liz wanted to pump her fist. Instead, she tapped on her keyboard. Before the cyclists left, Liz called, "Sew Welcome is hosting a quilting party tonight around seven. We love to have guests, whether you sew or not."

"Maybe. Stephanie and I were thinking about going to Fort Wayne tonight," Jessi said.

Kandy paused. "My grandma used to make quilts. I've always wanted to see how it's done."

"Please join us. Naomi, my baker friend, is bringing her to-die-for cinnamon rolls."

"You have a lot of friends who can cook. That pie yesterday was incredible."

Not exactly a compliment from Trent. But she'd take it.

"Can't I come to the party too?" Jason stuck out his lip.

"Certainly." Liz laughed. "Male quilters have attended before, and guys are more than welcome. But FYI, Naomi usually brings enough for breakfast the next day."

"Let's go." Trent headed out the front door with the others in his wake.

Kandy smiled and waved at Liz.

What a smile. Liz hoped the young woman would find more reasons to smile today.

She shouldn't be so glad the bikers had slept past breakfast hour—though perhaps extra breathing space this morning wouldn't hurt anyone.

Liz finished reviewing her bills, grabbed her cleaning caddy, and headed upstairs to help Sarah tidy the cyclists' rooms. As she expected, young Mrs. Clean had already finished the two bathrooms—Liz didn't mind that at all—and was making beds.

Liz greeted her and plopped pillows on the bed. Normally, she sensed a smile behind the nineteen-year-old's quiet demeanor, even if her face didn't show it. But this morning, Sarah's blonde brows hovered over her eyes, a sign that one of her headaches had announced its arrival. "Are you feeling all right?"

"I'm okay." Sarah hesitated. "I knocked on the door of the Somewhere in Time Room earlier, and Mr. Brummett answered. I thought he said, 'Come in.' Apparently, he did not."

Great. At least Sarah hadn't surprised Trent. "How embarrassing for you."

"Oh no." The maid's round cheeks flushed pink. "He was . . . fully dressed. But Mr. Brummett became quite annoyed, though I apologized for my mistake."

That sounded more like Trent than Jason. Liz said, "He seemed perfectly fine just a few minutes ago. Didn't mention a word about it. I wonder what set Jason off."

Sarah shook her head. "I have no idea. He appeared to be taking medication. He was pouring capsules from a bottle onto the dresser."

"Maybe he had a headache too." *No wonder, rooming with Trent.* Liz shrugged and patted Sarah's shoulder. "At any rate, it was a simple mistake, for which you apologized. You're my right-hand helper. Don't let it bother you." She grabbed her caddy again and lowered her voice. "Let's finish these rooms, and hopefully, the other guests will wake up soon."

Eventually, they did. Coffee and plates of pumpkin and cranberry bread Liz had left for them in the dining room helped bring them to life.

Big Berky seemed almost pleasant as he led the group to the town square to set up their booth. "Busy day today," he told Liz. "We won't be back for coffee hour."

Liz couldn't help feeling relieved.

In the past, she'd looked forward to spending that special time with her guests.

Today, she'd just as soon drink coffee by herself.

3

To Liz's surprise, all the biker girls showed up at the quilting party that evening. Sadie, having donned her black leather outfit for the occasion, must have encouraged them to attend. Mary Ann welcomed Honey, Pixie, and Shine the way she welcomed everyone—as if they'd come to a family reunion. The Sew Welcome owners introduced the other Material Girls: Naomi; seventyish Opal Ringenberg, who greeted them with her usual quiet dignity; and twenty-something Caitlyn Ross.

Caitlyn, a Material Girl? Liz saw the bikers' eyebrows go up. With her red-streaked hair, silver nose stud, and butterfly neck tattoo, Caitlyn looked like one of them. Yet she hung out with older women who made quilts?

Liz grinned inwardly. Caitlyn, a nurse, actually disliked motorcycles. She'd treated too many injuries associated with them. But no one would have guessed that. Friendly Caitlyn connected with the bikers, as she did with everyone. "Sadie said you might be too busy to come. Great that you could join us."

"We all needed some girl time." Shine laughed, white teeth gleaming against her dark skin. "Besides, we could smell those cinnamon rolls the second we walked in the door." She glanced around the spacious room, with its shelves of colorful fabric, large table, and row of sewing machines. Big windows framed the muted colors of the aged maple trees outside, lit by old-fashioned streetlamps. "This is one awesome room."

Pixie collapsed into the nearest rocking chair of a grouping where the Material Girls did handwork.

"Low blood sugar? We can take care of that." Naomi began handing out platefuls of warm rolls topped with gooey icing.

Good grief. Liz's mouth watered. *Those are the size of pot holders!* A universal "mmmm" filled the room as they gathered at the table. Liz followed with a tray of coffee and herbal teas. "I imagine organizing a major ride takes a great deal of work."

"Once Berky starts something, we have to talk him into taking even short breaks." Honey frowned. "I saw cute shops around the town square. And there's this booth close to ours that had awesome jewelry. But no. Berky's in charge of this ride, so we had to prepare everything for Saturday and check out every inch of the route." She sighed. "After dinner, Berky wanted to take another ride, a long one. I'd had enough."

The others nodded.

"Well, just relax tonight." Liz was trying to think of how to shift the conversation to a more positive subject when Kandy showed up, followed shortly by Miriam and Liz's aunt Ruth. More introductions were made, more refreshments distributed, and more chatty conversations flavored the evening. Miriam's and Aunt Ruth's Amish dresses and Kapps mingled with the others' leather, lace, leggings, and jeans.

Thank goodness, things were going well—except that Kandy and Honey remained on opposite sides of the room, as if a line had been drawn down the middle.

On the other hand, perhaps that would keep things going well. Having avoided another challenging coffee hour, Liz preferred not to deal with a similar mood here.

Trent, sporting a fedora, had left with guy cycling friends from another club. Yet it seemed that Mr. Ego held sway over this party as if he were present.

Without thinking, Liz gulped throat-searing coffee. *Why am I letting this guy get to me?* Soothing her mouth with ice water, she knew the answer. He reminded her way too much of Matt. The thought that two such self-centered guys existed on the same planet made her want to run away screaming—after eating a third cinnamon roll.

Instead, she said to Mary Ann, "Why don't we show everyone the quilt we're going to auction off at the Harvest Festival?"

"Good idea." Mary Ann pulled the quilt from the stacked cubbyholes along one wall. She and Sadie unfolded it.

Mouths fell open, then oohs, aahs, and chuckles arose as Sadie, in a faithful imitation of Vanna White, displayed its features.

Though Liz had seen the quilt every week, she still marveled at its mosaic complexity. It featured a schoolhouse surrounded by brilliantly hued trees with faceless Amish children walking through a pumpkin field. Faceless, Liz knew, in order to avoid offending Amish friends, who considered portraits of any kind prideful.

Miriam would never own such a colorful bedcover, as her bishop would consider it frivolous. Yet she appreciated the art others created for their homes. "Your fabrics and patterns work so well in that quilt." Miriam, an expert herself, gave it a smiling seal of approval. "Not too busy, despite all the variety. Perfect balance."

"It looks like the schoolhouse down my road!" Aunt Ruth exclaimed.

Sadie nodded. "Actually, we designed it from a photo I took there last fall."

"We're hoping it will inspire major bids to help fund Clothe Our Kids this winter." Mary Ann talked about the local charity, which assisted low-income families with their children's clothing costs.

"Somebody will pay big bucks for that," Pixie declared.

"I wish I could buy it for my mother." Kandy sounded wistful. "She loves quilts."

"This is the Christmas quilt we're working on now." Mary Ann showed them a sketch of it, which featured a Nativity scene.

As the others gathered around it, Liz noted that Honey and Kandy apparently had forgotten to maintain their distance.

Sadie-Vanna pointed out several motifs: baby Jesus, Mary, and the stable. "See? Jesus is almost finished." Suddenly reverent, she touched the figure. "When we work on a biblical quilt, we always finish Jesus first."

"That sketch looks like a stained glass window." Kandy lowered her voice as if in a church.

"Exactly the effect we want." Mary Ann swept them all with her irresistible smile. "Would you like to help us work on it this evening?"

As if choreographed, Liz's young guests stepped back.

Pixie, who resembled her biker name, waved it away with tiny hands. "Don't let me even touch it."

Honey shook her head. "I can't remember the last time I threaded a needle."

"You don't have to." Caitlyn motioned her toward the sketch. "Yeah, the figures are harder to do. But there's a lot of sky in this picture composed of rectangles, all different colors of blue. And the stars are made of little diamonds of fabric. We need someone to press the pieces Sadie and Opal will cut for it. And anyone who can sew a straight seam can man the machines."

"Well, maybe . . ." Kandy moved closer.

Unfortunately, Honey did too, and the rivals bumped elbows. They flinched as if they'd touched fire.

Opal slipped between them and edged Kandy to the cutting table. "Come help me with the patterns."

Mary Ann steered Honey to the ironing boards.

Everyone else scattered, chattering again.

Liz, basting pieces for an angel figure, sneaked occasional looks at the adversaries. Though their Material Girl mentors managed to keep them busy most of the time, Honey sent supercilious smiles toward Kandy whenever she could catch her eye. Kandy ignored the biker's existence until Honey, describing the Hog Wild Ride route to Mary Ann, raised her melting voice just loud enough so Kandy could hear: "I'm not sure what we'll do Saturday about those bicycle riders crossing our route. It'll mess up our whole ride."

Kandy tensed but continued pulling pins from the pieces Opal had cut.

"Trent will figure out something." Honey's long eyelashes fluttered. "He's so smart. Cute too."

They didn't call her Honey only because of her hair.

Kandy stuck pins into her cushion as if stabbing a voodoo doll.

Liz, sitting in a rocking chair nearby, said, "Surely something can be worked out."

"Maybe it would be better for everyone if bikers and cyclists stayed out of each other's territories," Kandy said coldly. The knifelike gaze she shot at Honey took Liz's breath away. Obviously, Kandy was talking about more than roads.

"Now, that would be a shame," the biker chick cooed, "when we have such a wonderful chance to get to know each other."

"*Wonderful?*" Kandy flushed fiery red.

For a minute, Liz thought Kandy would throw a punch at Honey. Her dark side almost hoped Kandy would.

But the cyclist deliberately turned her back on her foe and returned to her work.

Sadie plunged into a stand-up performance of her worst jokes, so lame that everyone had to laugh.

Everyone but Kandy. Finishing her task, she approached Liz and whispered, "Thanks for inviting me tonight. I saw a little theater downtown, and I think I'll take in a movie to relax. Would you thank Mary Ann and Sadie for me?"

"Sure." Liz patted Kandy's shoulder, then accompanied her from Sew Welcome to the rotunda. As Kandy's blonde braid vanished out the front door, Liz tried to think of solutions to the women's conflict.

Short of deporting Trent to Siberia, she came up empty.

The group made substantial progress on the Christmas quilt. After Kandy left, everyone continued to get along famously, though Honey often grabbed the spotlight. Sweetly, of course.

Are you and Trent two of a kind? And with Matt, three of a kind? Liz shuddered.

Whatever did Kandy see in Trent anyway? Surely there were other hunky, charming racers riding Saturday . . .

Chiding herself for matchmaking, Liz chatted with Aunt Ruth as she basted, basking in her aunt's resemblance to her late mother. She had the same fathomless gray eyes and a similar sideways smile. For a while, the warmth they shared helped insulate Liz from her earlier thoughts.

Before long, though, the older woman asked Miriam to take her home. "Phoebe and Tabitha are coming tomorrow to help me make apple cakes for the festival. Five o'clock comes early."

"I still have baking to do too." Miriam rose from her rocking chair. "And the horses have to go to work early tomorrow."

Soon after they left, friends newly arrived for the festival called Shine on her cell. Did she and the other biker chicks want to meet them in Marion? The three decided the evening—especially the cinnamon rolls—had revived them, and they would go. They finished their projects and helped straighten the sewing room before thanking the Material Girls and leaving.

"I wouldn't have pushed them out the door, but that worked well for me." Opal gathered her belongings. "I still have much to do."

Mary Ann, Sadie, and Naomi gratefully called it quits as well.

First, though, Mary Ann cornered Liz in the kitchen. "You've got your hands full, don't you?" She leveled a knowing gaze at her.

"Well, yes, but that comes with running an inn." Liz tried to chuckle. "Not everybody 'gets' everybody else."

"You can't make everyone happy." Mary Ann patted her shoulder. "Take time to enjoy the festival."

"Oh, I will. Jackson and I are checking out downtown tomorrow. He says that going before the official festival opening is the best way to experience it."

Mary Ann nodded. "Good plan. Fewer crowds. Easier to spend time together."

Liz detected the wedding-bells note in her friend's approval. "Don't marry us off yet."

"I won't have to. Jackson will take care of that. You'll see." Mary Ann grinned wickedly and departed.

Thank goodness, Caitlyn was staying for a post-session gab. Happy to be single, the youngest Material Girl could talk with Liz about guys without making a quantum leap to matrimony.

Caitlyn had boiled water in Liz's brass kettle for tea, knowing Liz preferred it, though microwaving was faster. Having brewed rose hips for herself and lemon ginger for Liz, Caitlyn said, "I thought Honey was going to Marion with the others."

"She did." Liz didn't really want to talk about Honey.

Caitlyn handed Liz her mug. "I can't be absolutely positive because I spotted her by your safety lights in the backyard, but I'm pretty sure I just saw Honey wander toward the lake a few minutes ago."

"I guess she changed her mind." Liz shrugged. "If I'd ridden umpteen miles already today, my backside would be ready for a walk, not another ride."

"Not sure it had anything to do with that. She was with a guy."

"Oh. Big Berky must have returned sooner than he expected." During quilting chitchat, Liz had heard the young women say that the biker guys, annoyed at their lack of enthusiasm, had planned to make a late night of it. However, a twinge of uneasiness nudged her, insistent as Beans.

"Maybe." A quizzical look crossed Caitlyn's face. "But Big Berky looks like his name, right? As in, huge?"

Liz stopped mid-sip. "Yeah."

"Well, this guy was kind of tall. But he was slim. Didn't see his face, but I loved his fedora."

Trent.

Feeling like a voyeur, Liz slipped into the four-season room. A light near the lake's pier shone enough for Liz to see a couple passing it, the man wearing a hat. Following the lakeside path, they disappeared into the woods.

Caitlyn, at her elbow, sipped tea but said nothing.

Liz closed her eyes. The festival had already brought more excitement to the Olde Mansion Inn than she'd anticipated.

But given what they had just witnessed, Liz hadn't seen nothin' yet.

4

Liz had dragged herself to bed last night like a hundred-year-old lady. But this magic morning, she felt like a college girl again.

Just enough buttery sunshine melted into the crisp October air. Pleasant Creek's clock tower, a massive limestone edifice surrounded by flower beds of jewel-colored chrysanthemums, sang out the time in its commanding melody.

Though the festival would not officially open until evening, most of the vendors were already in full operation. Crackling fires popped big, black kettles of popcorn and simmered others full of bubbling apple butter. They spread a gentle autumn-flavored haze across the downtown square. Craft tents of every kind bloomed in each direction, bursting with handmade pottery, quilts, rugs, furniture, and clothing, as well as some of the most delectable food in the Midwest.

Besides all that, Liz walked, talked, and laughed with the best-looking bachelor in Pleasant Creek, their linked hands swinging in carefree rhythm.

Did it get any better than that?

Well, no. As Liz and Jackson turned a corner, she spotted Trent, wearing his signature fedora. But he wasn't wooing Honey. And definitely not Kandy.

He was romancing a lovely Amish girl. Tucked cozily between tents, the couple stood a proper distance apart with hands barely touching, but the girl glowed as if struck by lightning.

Liz wanted to snatch apples from a nearby ruby-red pile and pelt some sense into Trent. *Though if I threw the whole pile at him, would it do any good?*

Jackson halted. "Um, is something wrong?"

Liz dropped his hand, trying not to grit her teeth. "One of my guests has caused some . . . tension the past day or two. He appears to be trying to stir up more trouble here."

Jackson followed her gaze. "I can believe that."

"You can?"

"I don't remember his name, but I remember him. Star cyclist. A real lady-killer. In past years, he played the field around here. Who is he?"

"Trent Cleveland." Liz wished she'd never heard of the man.

"He broke up at least two engaged couples. Looks like he's at it again."

Liz's hand went to her mouth. "That girl's engaged?"

"Yes. That's Amy Lapp." Jackson set his jaw. "She's engaged to Nathan Troyer, who's related to my family. I'm invited to the wedding in December."

As if on cue, a tall, lanky young Amish man emerged from a nearby tent. Though his face had assumed the frozen expression many in his community wore when provoked, Nathan's eyes glinted like steel bearings as he accosted his scarlet-faced fiancée.

She turned white, though, as Nathan spoke to Trent. Typical for the Amish, the boy did not raise his voice, so Liz couldn't hear what he said.

Trent shrugged off Nathan's anger with his usual insolent grin and strutted off. To seek more feminine prey?

Liz couldn't bear to look at Trent. She didn't want to watch the couple's confrontation, either, so she aimed her gaze across the street. A tall, middle-aged Amish man with a marked resemblance to Nathan presided over a tent full of pumpkins, gourds, and cornstalks. He wore the future groom's expression too. His faded wife, her eyes averted, fussed over jars of jam, her mouth working. Rose Stoltzfus, apparently helping them, retreated toward the rear of the tent.

"Noah and Kezia Troyer, Nathan's parents," Jackson said. His hazel eyes, normally warm and twinkling, held a glimmer of sorrow. "I hope Nathan and Amy can work this out. He and his family don't deserve double pain."

Liz stared. "Double pain?"

"Trent broke up Nathan's first engagement too."

She gasped, speechless.

"Yes, that wonderful guy swept Nathan's fiancée Susannah Koenig off her feet. Of course, she meant nothing to Trent." Jackson gestured toward the cyclist's departing back. "But the damage was done. She ended up marrying someone else."

While such occurrences complicated any social scene, they injured the close-knit Amish community even more. Liz said, "You're the mayor. Can't you tell Trent he has to get out of town by sunset?"

Jackson's thin chuckle sounded nothing like his usual hearty laugh. "Believe me, if I could, I would." Frowning, he ran a hand through his well-groomed brown hair, standing it on end. "I really don't like his staying at your inn."

"As if I do! But I can't kick him out. I'm in the hospitality business, remember?"

Jackson searched her face. "Be careful. That guy mesmerizes women—"

"You think *I'll* fall for that scuzzball?" Liz couldn't believe it.

"No, no." Jackson backpedaled quickly, but his gaze jumped sideways.

Liz drew herself to her full height. "First, I'm almost old enough to be his mother. Second, if Mr. Wonderful tries his moves on me, I'll kick him out all right. To the next state."

"Good." A small, satisfied smile touched Jackson's lips. But he didn't attempt to take her hand again.

Was he jealous? Alternately flattered and annoyed, Liz didn't know what else to say.

Jackson fell back on the time-honored male method of dealing with difficult situations—eating. He took her to lunch at an Amish booth that featured homemade sausage sandwiches and hot apple betty.

"Why does every celebration in Indiana require me to gain five pounds?" Liz said, munching away. She didn't feel *that* much regret.

"Hoosier law." Jackson took a huge bite of his sandwich. "We wouldn't want to be lawbreakers, would we?"

Trying to recapture the day's earlier carefree spirit, they viewed what was called the Young Fair exhibits—animal husbandry and crafts by the area's children. Then they cheered Sadie's winning a champion ribbon for her bread-and-butter pickles. Still, their silences grew longer and, well, awkward. Liz was about to use her guests as an excuse to conclude their date.

But Jackson pointed to a tent that rented bicycles. "Perfect! Come on. Let's try a tandem."

"But I've never—"

"Me either. But I've always wanted to, haven't you?" He caught Liz's hand and melted her with his little-boy look. "It'll be fun."

Maybe he was right. After today's brief interlude, running her inn would consume Liz. Running his furniture store and booth would devour his time. They both rode regularly with their bicycle club, but perhaps a quiet ride, just the two of them, in the nearby countryside would relax them again. Besides, why turn down new adventures?

Liz raised her chin. "Let's do it!"

Jackson knew the booth's proprietor, a wiry Amish man who conducted a thriving business in Pleasant Creek, as many in his community used bikes as regular transportation.

"If I were you, I'd wheel it out of the square on foot and stay on back roads," he advised as they donned rented helmets. "The streets and even the county roads are crowded, and riding a tandem's different from a single."

Jackson nodded but only wheeled the bike out of the man's sight, then checked out the gears and brakes. "This bike has more low gears than mine, but I doubt we'll need them. Flat land has its advantages."

He pulled water bottles from their racks. "Could you fill these up at the comfort station?"

"Uh, sure." Liz took them to the central area that included restrooms and water coolers. When she returned, he'd parked himself on the front seat.

You could have asked me if I'd *like to ride on the front.*

Jackson's grin of anticipation stretched so wide that Liz decided not to raise the issue.

She replaced the bottles and hopped on the back. "Do we pedal automatically at the same speed?"

He showed her that yes, they did. They fiddled with the bike a minute or two until Jackson pronounced them ready to take off.

Were they? Jackson's broad back blocked her view. She'd have to ride blind. Her handlebars held no brakes, no gears. She couldn't stop or steer this bike.

"We have to start at exactly the same time," Jackson instructed as they positioned their feet on the pedals. "Ready?"

"Ready." Only she wasn't. She craned her neck, trying to see around Jackson.

The tandem took off like an unbridled horse. Her feet tried to stop it.

Jackson yelled. The bike veered, barely missing a trio of trash cans. He slammed on the brakes.

Her helmeted head slammed into him. She managed to plant her feet on solid ground before the bike tilted. Good old solid ground.

Rubbing his shoulder blades where he'd been butted, Jackson turned and said, "Are you okay?"

Just hunky-dory. "I guess . . . I wasn't quite ready."

Liz heard half-smothered chuckles on both sides. Some spectator haw-hawed. "Hey, Mayor! Cops'll get you for reckless driving!"

Several Amish passersby were polite enough to attempt to hide their grins.

Jackson took a long drink from his water bottle, then said, "When we're riding a tandem, we have to be on the same page."

Yeah, your page. Immediately, Liz chided herself. She should have told him she wasn't ready. "You're right. I'm used to seeing the traffic ahead and acting accordingly. When I couldn't, my instinct kicked in. I tried to brake, though I don't have any brakes."

She attempted to laugh. He attempted to laugh.

Neither sounded terribly convincing.

He said, "Well, do you want to try again?"

Liz had never been a quitter. She didn't want to start now, especially with Jackson scrutinizing her with those magnetic eyes. "Sure."

He turned around and poised for the start. "Are you ready now?"

Ignoring their lingering fan club, she positioned her right foot firmly on the pedal. "Ready as I'll ever be."

Jackson intoned, "One. Two. Three. Go!"

Still wobbly, they managed to navigate the bike past a row of portable toilets without knocking them over. Liz tried not to imagine the local paper's headline if they had: Tipsy Mayor Topples Toilets.

What if someone had been taking pictures of this whole scenario? *So much for getting away from it all.*

Once they'd ridden several blocks to a residential area, though, Liz's tight shoulder muscles began to loosen. They passed some of her favorite old houses, including mansions built during Indiana's prosperous natural-gas boom more than a century before. Such gracious old ladies, with their pillars, porches, gables, and cupolas, surrounded by venerable, colorful trees and blazing fire bush. She even liked the funky Victorian the owner had trimmed with violet, coral, and aqua.

Riding on the backseat, Liz didn't have to watch for traffic or shift gears. She did have to keep track of Jackson's shifts and try to anticipate his stops—good thing she was familiar with the town's stop signs. But this duo was actually riding in rhythm now. While she couldn't see Jackson's face, she could watch their self-made breeze running its fingers through his thick, shining hair, something she wouldn't mind doing herself.

He steered them down a dusty gravel road she wasn't familiar with that took them to the middle of nowhere. The tandem bounced and bounded over its uneven surface like an unshod colt, the ride taking its toll on her backside. Would she have time to shower again before coffee hour?

Her objections, however, lessened with the realization that the gravel was packed down, with minimal dust.

Plus, they were riding through one of the most picturesque areas she'd ever seen.

Old-fashioned, rustling corn shocks dotted Amish fields. A thousand pumpkins brightened another field, as if the sun had emptied a treasure chest of its gold onto the earth. A brook flowed peacefully alongside the road, its shallower waters chuckling over worn limestone and sandstone rocks. Jackson told her that was *the* Pleasant Creek.

Trees with gilt-edged, flaming leaves hovered over it, reflected in the water. Small groves of golden tulip poplars adorned the opposite shore. Two "sticks" suddenly flew across the stream, long legs trailing after widespread wings. Herons! Liz had never seen them that close, winging across the road ahead with a grace she would not have suspected.

"Used to canoe here when I was a boy," Jackson said over his shoulder, and she realized he was showing her something special.

Her heart beat a little faster as they rode through a dusky, one-lane covered bridge built in 1898, according to the figures painted over its entrance. The bridge was paved only with wooden planks that creaked as the bike crossed them. Slivers of light and sparkly water shone through gaps in the bridge floor. Surely this thing was sturdy enough to handle their weight. But what if—?

"Old bridge. Might collapse any moment." Jackson flung a wicked grin over his shoulder.

Liz hoped the twilight inside the bridge wouldn't let him see her sweat.

She smothered a sigh of relief as they bumped onto the gravel road, back to open fields and everlasting cerulean sky.

But new gravel had been laid on the next few miles, slogging their progress. Sneezing violently, Liz choked on dust from the few cars that passed them.

"Sorry!" Jackson yelled. "I'll find us some blacktop."

Fortunately, he knew this area from county line to county line. Before long, they rolled onto smooth pavement, and Liz reveled in the pristine, lovely countryside once more.

Until three pairs of canine eyes spotted their bike from a farmhouse porch. An enormous German shepherd, a hound, and a small, yappy dog sprinted toward them, baying and snarling as if protecting their domain from the devil.

Adrenaline shot through Liz, and she pedaled faster than she thought possible.

Jackson, however, hit the brakes.

Her knees jammed her chin. She tasted blood.

The bike rocked. Jackson bellowed at the animals.

The dogs froze.

"Pedal!" Liz shrieked. "Fast! Fast!"

"No," Jackson said in a maddeningly calm voice. "Don't show fear."

He pedaled at a leisurely pace, not showing fear, while three sets of growling, bared incisors followed, seemingly inches from Liz's ankles.

She wanted to leap off the bike and run, but that would only make her a more convenient meal. In this case, fast food would not prove fast enough.

"They'll go back home when we reach the end of their property," Jackson said in the same level tone.

With her luck, their master owned half the county. Liz forced aching joints and muscles to push the pedals a little farther. She really wanted them both to survive.

So she could kill him.

Sure enough, at the next crossroads, the dogs' lope lessened to a trot, then halted. All three watched, growls still reverberating in their throats, as Jackson and Liz continued their ride along the smooth road.

Jackson's backward glance and grin said, *See?*

She saw all right.

The near-perfect ride back to the inn cooled her inner volcano enough so that Liz didn't erupt when they pulled up near the inn's front door. But if Jackson was expecting hugs and kisses as they went their separate ways, he'd better think again.

At least they'd learned to stop the tandem successfully. She dropped her feet from the pedals just after he braked, slipped from the seat, and removed her helmet. She clasped her helmet strap around her handlebars so he could return it. "Sorry to make you walk the bike back to the rental tent, but I really have to grab a shower, then prep for coffee hour. Thanks for lunch. And for the, um, ride."

He'd turned to face her, his smile fading. "Is something . . . wrong?"

I can't believe *you!* "Oh no. Nothing that a little major orthopedic surgery couldn't fix."

Jackson stared. "Did the dogs hurt you?"

She snapped, "No! But they could have bitten my legs off, for all you knew. You were too busy showing no fear!"

"But that's what you do when a dog chases you." His eyes ignited, then blazed. "No bike will outrun a dog. You can't panic."

"Easy for you to say. Dogs never chase the *front* of a bike!"

"Miss Eckardt?" Sarah poked her head out the front door. "I'm sorry to interrupt, but the coffeemaker doesn't seem to be working."

Wonderful. Thirty minutes to find a substitute.

And she and Jackson had been yelling at each other like teenagers on Main Street. Liz fidgeted. "I'm sorry I raised my voice. It really was a . . . nice day. Most of it."

"Yeah." Jackson looked away. "Well, I'd better get this thing back to the rental." He turned the bike around, running over his foot. "Ouch. Blast!"

She hurried inside, both glad and sorry to conclude their afternoon.

They had planned to ride the leisurely twenty-mile Kappel Apple Ride after the racers took off, but Jackson hadn't mentioned it. And not so strangely, Jackson hadn't said anything about going out again. Liz sighed. The day had plunged downhill surprisingly fast.

Usually, she looked forward to coffee hour with her guests.

But today, only if another coffeemaker somehow showed up—and Trent didn't.

5

Liz, shooting the breeze with Shine, Pixie, and Scooby, heard Trent before she saw him. He was laughing. But his laugh always sounded like a taunt.

One look at Kandy's face as the two entered the sitting room and Liz knew he was using her for target practice. To Liz's surprise, Kandy didn't slump into her usual blank-eyed silence. Eyes hard as sapphires, she snapped at him under her breath, then joined Stephanie and Jessi at the beverage bar, using the extra coffeemaker Liz had borrowed from Naomi.

Kandy's anger didn't appear to disturb Trent. He stationed himself close to the platter—with this hard-riding group, Liz had dispensed with a mere plate—of chocolate chip cookies. "These are awesome," he said as he dispatched half a dozen. "Main reason why I came back."

Honey sauntered in, and Trent's eyes lit on her. She had a red-carpet walk that drew Trent like—well, like a bee to honey. He encircled her slim waist with his muscular arm, and they melded.

Liz, now mingling with the women cyclists, wanted to close her eyes. Face ablaze, Kandy strode across the room. "Knock it off, Trent!"

One part of Liz yelled a silent, *Get him, girl!* The other part backed away from the raging Nordic princess who seemed to have doubled in height.

Uneasiness flashed across Trent's face. Then his laugh returned. "What is your problem? Honey's a special friend." He sounded almost righteous. "You and I may be dating, but you have to understand—"

"We're not dating," Kandy spat, "and I understand perfectly. You wanted another chance. I gave you one. You haven't lasted the afternoon. We're done."

"Honey!" Just inside the door, Big Berky glowered, hands clenched in hamlike fists. "Where have you been?"

Liz had been trying to think of something that would help the situation. But at that moment, she simply donned an invisible helmet and braced herself for whatever was coming.

Honey crossed her arms. "Don't speak to me in that tone, Berky Parker. You don't have to know where I am every minute. It's not like I'm your Harley."

If Kandy hadn't slumped, Berky did. "You know I don't think of you like that. I sure don't own you. But I thought—"

"She was with Trent, Berky." Kandy flung the words like a challenge. "You're a nice guy and deserve better than Honey. If you're smart, you'll walk—no, run—and leave her in the dust, just like I'm leaving Trent." She turned to Liz. "I'm staying tonight. My chances are good to win the race tomorrow, and I'm going to do just that. I'm sorry, but after I win I'm outta here."

Liz opened her mouth, but before she could speak, Kandy marched from the room, blonde head high.

"You're a jerk." Jessi glared at Trent as she and Stephanie followed their friend.

Berky left without a word.

Jason, who was just entering, wisely moved aside as the big man plunged through the door. "What's going on, Trent?" He looked from his roommate to Honey to Liz and the remaining bikers, all of whom remained silent.

Trent laughed again but with a little less moxie. "Oh, Kandy's fussing about nothing, as usual."

Nothing? Liz risked a glance at Honey. Her rosebud mouth maintained its sweet poutiness, but her finely arched brows rose almost to her hairline.

Disgust flickered across Jason's face, but he headed for the refreshments without further comment.

Surprisingly, Beans followed on his heels. Had the quarrels disturbed and disengaged him from his rug? Liz hadn't seen him this active in months.

Minus Trent and Honey, who had retreated to a love seat, the others welcomed the dog as if he were the president. Liz knelt and patted him too. After all the brouhaha, Beans's doggy smile and wagging tail warmed her heart.

Maybe wagging a little too fast? Beans nosed Liz's guests until tiny Pixie almost stumbled.

Liz grabbed his collar. "What on earth has gotten into you, Beans?"

"He's looking for Bulldog," Scooby said. "Bulldog and peanut butter."

Of course.

"Sorry, boy." Shine scratched behind his ears. "Bulldog had to do stuff at the booth. He'll be back later."

"Beans shouldn't expect peanut butter every time he shows up." Liz had to half-drag the dog from the sitting room. "Come on, Beans. Let's go see Sadie. Want to see Sadie, boy?"

When he realized where Liz was leading him, Beans, who knew Sadie was a softer touch, allowed Liz to pull him through the door of the store.

While Sadie coddled the dog and gave him a treat, Mary Ann took one look at Liz and made her sit. Since no customers were around right now, Liz knew her friend would ferret out the details of her woes.

Sure enough, Mary Ann said, "Another fun coffee hour?"

"The worst." Liz held her head in her hands. "Maybe I should have bought a B&B in a more peaceful spot. Like the Ukraine."

Mary Ann and Sadie listened to her problems, clucking their tongues sympathetically at all the right places.

At the end of her recital, Mary Ann murmured, "Well, boys and girls will be boys and girls."

"I guess you're right." No relationship was perfect. Certainly, she and Jackson had moved past the honeymoon phase. The word sent heat shooting up Liz's face.

Mary Ann cocked her head. "Is something else wrong?"

Nothing missed her friend's sharp eyes. Liz shrugged. "Right now, everything."

Mary Ann pursed her carefully lipsticked mouth but did not press Liz. "Your guests probably have too much spare time. The race and ride tomorrow will use up some of that competitive energy."

"Don't let 'em back you into a corner," Sadie advised. "Tell them to play nice or else!"

"Or else what?"

"Or else you'll paint 'em with peanut butter and let Beans loose."

Liz laughed. She couldn't help picturing the fun of chasing Trent with an open jar. That made her feel better too.

"Ooh, evil thoughts." Mary Ann waggled her eyebrows. "I can tell your wheels are turning."

"But only thoughts. They'll stay that way." Liz sighed. "Actually, Kandy and Big Berky have already gone their separate ways. But Trent and Honey are still at coffee hour." She really didn't want to return to the sitting room, but someone had to pick up the pieces.

"I'll go with you." Mary Ann rose from her stool.

Leaving Sadie to mind the store, they marched to the sitting room. But all her guests had disappeared.

"Those lovebirds knew they were in trouble," Mary Ann said. "That you were going to bring back the big guns."

Liz chuckled. "Never underestimate the power of a grandma."

"Before I go to the pie tent, I'll help you clean up." Mary Ann started to gather used mugs and napkins.

"I can do this." Liz snatched them from her. "You have quite a night ahead of you." Mary Ann headed the committee that baked a seven-foot latticed apple pie every year for the festival.

"Nothing I can't handle." Mary Ann smiled. "Actually, I really enjoy it. Naomi and Opal are such a help, and all the cooks want to make the best crust and filling possible."

"Peeling all those apples—how many do you use?"

"Oh, sixteen bushels, give or take. We always use at least some apples from the Kappel Apple Tree."

Liz knew she spoke of the tree—documented to have been planted by Johnny Appleseed—near a small church or *Kappel* (German for "chapel"). The first bicycle race had begun there a hundred years before, and it would start and finish there tomorrow.

"We already finished the filling," Mary Ann continued. "Just have to do the crust and bake it overnight at Naomi's." She made the massive undertaking sound like a junior 4-H project. "Of course, I'll stay in the back room to ensure it bakes properly."

Just cooking breakfast and baking cookies for coffee hour sometimes pushed Liz's culinary skills to the limit. The mere thought of this gigantic pie project made her want to take a nap.

Mary Ann caught her eye. "But I don't have to live a soap opera, as you have the past couple of days. I think you're due a little peace and quiet and maybe a cup of hot cider in the four-season room."

That sounded so nice. "Maybe." Or perhaps she'd sneak off to her favorite backyard bench, hidden from the world in a little grove of giant lilac bushes. From there, she could watch the sun go down over the lake and regain her equilibrium.

The latter formula for recovery worked so well that she skipped cooking supper for herself and remained on the bench, wrapped in a comfy plaid football blanket. Liz stayed until the sun dipped its toes in the chilly water, then tumbled into the depths of the lake.

Yet God will help the sun shine tomorrow. She prayed for equal resiliency.

Both Liz and the dawn awakened at the same time the next morning, refreshed and ready to refresh others. She cooked an unusually large breakfast, including plenty of cyclist-friendly baked oatmeal, dried-fruit compote, nuts, and fresh fruit, as well as the eggs, potatoes, and breakfast meats craved by the bikers.

Trent and Honey had decided to eat elsewhere, which didn't bother Liz one bit. Apparently, the others liked that arrangement as well. Conversation about the day buzzed. A few kindly gibes flew back and forth between the cyclists and bikers. Even Big Berky, alone and drowning his sorrows in heaps of bacon, couldn't hide a smile behind his beard.

"Great spread, Liz," Jason said. The others murmured in agreement. Such a nice guy. *Kandy, why don't you look his way?*

But the Nordic princess's anger appeared to have hardened to an invisible shell, insulating her from everyone. Sitting on the edge of her chair, she attacked her food as if preparing for battle.

They all seemed focused this morning, ready to ride. Mary Ann had been right. But later, after someone else rode faster and better, would goodwill continue among the racers? Would Trent return to devour chocolate chip cookies, gloat about his victory, and detonate coffee hour again?

She pushed away her paranoia as they rose to leave. "Have a great ride, everybody!"

"You too," Shine said, and the others echoed her good wishes.

Liz intended to, Jackson or no Jackson. She and Sarah whisked dirty dishes into the kitchen in record time. Liz left them in the capable hands of her maid and the dishwasher and went to her quarters to change into cycling shorts. She emerged from the inn just in time to see Honey ride off with a different biker group, presumably to the Hog Wild Ride in Wildton. She'd arrived in Pleasant Creek riding behind Big Berky. Had she rented, borrowed, or bought her own motorcycle?

In the parking lot, Sadie started Pink Penelope's engine as Berky and the other bikers fired up their motorcycles.

Somewhere, sometime, Liz had heard a Beach Boys song about a "little old lady from Pasadena." That old lady couldn't have begun to compete with Sadie. Her magenta-and-black leather outfit gleamed with a thousand metal studs. Huge sequined magenta roses bloomed on her back, on her leggings. With today's sunlight, Liz hoped Sadie wouldn't blind the riders behind her.

At first, Liz thought Sadie's grandson rode in her small sidecar. But spunky little Sam wouldn't have tolerated all that pink.

Beans.

He wore a matching getup, down to the roses. A little helmet. And Doggles!

Liz choked on her giggles. Though, officially, she was Beans's mistress, she'd given up real ownership to Sadie long ago.

The biker guys objected. "Beans looks like a girl." Big Berky's protests almost sounded like his normal bellow.

"He's so cute!" Pixie and Shine patted the dog.

Beans wagged at Bulldog, licking his chops hopefully.

"Here you are, boy." Bulldog handed the canine a sandwich. "Have a good ride, even if they've dressed you up like a sissy."

Beans, masculinity obviously undisturbed, dispatched it in two gulps.

"Come on. Let's ride!" Big Berky mounted his bike.

The women took their seats behind the guys, and the group thundered out of the parking lot and down Main Street.

Liz wheeled her bicycle from the garage and left, pausing near Sweet Everything.

Even if she'd been trying to find her way blind through town, she could have located Naomi's bakery. It was always fragrant, but today it fairly poured the luscious scent of apple pie into the brisk October morning. Though the pie would not finish baking until nearly noon, a line already snaked out the door, visitors staring with hungry eyes.

Note to self: Come here the second I'm done with my ride. Despite the size of the pie, it usually disappeared by late afternoon.

Liz rode to the nineteenth-century Kappel located near the town square. Although Pleasant Creek seemed too small to host a major race, it had grown into one of the most important time-trial competitions in the Midwest.

But Liz hadn't acquired the itch to race. Along with most local riders, she enjoyed cycling the easier twenty-mile route at her own speed.

First, though, the racers would take off. Liz pulled up near the steepled brick building and parked her bike in one of the temporary racks placed in the spacious churchyard. After she checked in at the registration table, she hurried to the starting area. Could she cheer for Trent?

Well, she'd do her best.

At least a hundred cyclists clumped in the churchyard, most dressed in sleek, colorful garb. Nibbling orange slices and granola bars, they discussed the present and past races.

Trent, clad in his signature gleaming silver and black, was surrounded by a harem of admirers. Liz circled away to avoid the sight.

Jason was talking to Caitlyn. Perhaps they'd known each other from other races. Liz's red-haired friend, wearing a white jersey with slashes of maroon, red, and black, stood out even in this crowd.

Liz couldn't comprehend wanting to ride a hundred miles. With any luck, she'd finish twenty without having to be hauled back in a SAG van.

Caitlyn called, "Hey, Liz! With everything going on at the inn, I wasn't sure you'd make it."

"I really wanted to ride today." *Really.* Liz said, "So you're actually going to do a century ride?"

"I hope so. Rode more than eighty miles last year before I begged a van to save my life." Caitlyn grinned. "No wonder they call them SAG vans. I was sagging so badly I could hardly climb in."

"You'll do great today," Jason assured her.

"I'm sure *you* will," Caitlyn said. "You do this all the time."

They introduced Liz to their fellow racers. Kandy, Stephanie, and Jessi joined the group. Kandy looked a little pale, but she seemed upbeat. Liz was enjoying their chat when the gleam of gold on a dark green helmet drew her eye.

The helmet Jackson wore when their club rode.

She'd known he was planning to ride today, so why did her stomach suddenly wobble like their rental tandem?

Its unease only worsened when he removed his helmet, and the sun scattered gold highlights through his hair.

"There's your handsome mayor." Caitlyn gave Liz a little shove.

Jackson, mistaking her movement toward him as voluntary, pushed his bike eagerly toward her.

Liz shook off her middle-school jitters and pasted a smile on her lips. "Hello, Jackson."

"Hello." He stopped, uncertainty hovering over his face.

Caitlyn waved him over. "Hey, Jackson! Come and meet my competition."

This group thing worked better than an alone conversation with him. Jackson turned on the charm, as usual, and by the time the men's race was announced, the women were giving Liz envious glances.

Easy for you to get all mushy about him. He didn't throw you to the dogs.

They all moved to the starting line, where the first cyclists—those at the top of the field, based on past races—would begin, thirty seconds apart for the timed race.

Trent was first.

All traces of the smarmy womanizer had vanished. Poised on his bike, Trent resembled a lean, powerful animal, lips pulled back from his teeth, unblinking eyes fixed on his goal.

Liz shook herself. She'd been staring. What was it about this guy?

Blushing, she felt Jackson's gaze on her. He'd been right. Trent did mesmerize women, even those who couldn't stand him.

"Want to move closer for a better view?" His quiet question contained a dozen barbs.

"No thanks." She tossed her hair from her face and noticed his hazel eyes had turned as green as his helmet.

When the timer signaled *go* and Trent rocketed from the starting line, she didn't cheer out loud. But she did cheer for Jason, who started third.

With Trent's departure, Jackson relaxed somewhat. Liz did too. They chatted with Caitlyn and the other women cyclists, Pleasant Creek friends, and Miriam, who was also going to ride the twenty-mile route.

"We Amish dislike competition," Miriam said in answer to one of the cyclists' questions, "but a bicycle ride on a beautiful morning with friends and neighbors? Certainly, that is something we can share."

However, several young men in Amish dress had attempted the race, wearing helmets instead of their usual broad-brimmed hats.

Her smile faltered when this was pointed out to her. "*Rumschpringe.* They have not yet decided whether to be baptized."

Jackson deftly changed the subject, engaging several bystanders in conversation. One couple turned out to be Trent's parents.

The man looked like Trent's grayer, heavier twin. Thankfully, he and his wife seemed as pleasant as their son was obnoxious. *Perhaps there's hope for Trent.*

They all yelled for Caitlyn, Kandy, and company when the women's race began. Finally, non-racing cyclists started their route.

Perhaps the magic of the perfect fall morning eased the taut, invisible cable between Liz and Jackson. And who wouldn't enjoy the fun of pedaling alongside friends? Generations of families, many of whom rode together every year, enjoyed the jaunt. Members of the Pleasant Creek cycling club kidded each other about their chances of finishing.

Liz and Miriam, riding side by side, caught up on family news. Miriam shook her head over her mischievous daughter Keturah's latest escapades. Liz shared memorized excerpts from Steve's last letter from Kosovo, where he was stationed. She loved riding with Miriam. But for the hundredth time, she wondered how Amish women could ride for miles wearing those long, flappy dresses.

Meanwhile, Jackson, always friendly, flashed his best smile as he greeted out-of-town riders in some of the best PR he did for Pleasant Creek. Liz even found herself bantering with the mayor, flinging back as good as she got, to the amusement of the others.

The miles passed so easily that their approach to the first SAG stop surprised her.

Not as much, though, as the scream of an ambulance behind them. She could hardly hear Jackson's shout to the riders to pull aside as its blinking lights lunged past them and careened around the curve ahead.

As usual, Liz breathed a prayer for those in need of help and their helpers. But she could not swallow a lump of foreboding that lodged in her throat.

One look at Jackson's face, furrowed with concern, only made it grow.

Jackson quickly assumed his leadership face and began to reassure the startled cyclists. "What a shame. But how thankful we are that we have good ambulance service, even out in the country. I'm sure they'll take good care of whoever needs help."

Dogs or no dogs, you are an excellent mayor. Liz couldn't help but admire his immediate concern for the people around him.

Calmed by Jackson's take-it-in-stride attitude, the others hopped back onto their bikes. As they pedaled the last mile to the SAG stop, Jackson surged ahead to encourage riders who clumped in nervous—and dangerous—bunches along the road.

Unfortunately, his optimism did not pan out. Not a single volunteer greeted them with a smile.

Liz's stomach knotted.

"What's up?" Jackson spoke to the stop's leader.

"A racer crashed somewhere between the fifty-mile stop and the finish line," the gray-haired man answered. "Doesn't sound good."

Jackson spent several minutes talking on his cell phone. He frowned deeply as he asked for the cyclists' and volunteers' attention. Gulping power drinks and munching on snacks, they circled as Jackson reviewed the incident. "We don't have many details yet. All we know is that the racer called 911 before veering off the road and crashing into a tree. Another cyclist found him there."

He glanced from rider to rider, his gaze resting on Liz. "I suggest we all pause to pray for Trent Cleveland."

6

"Trent?" Liz choked out.

How could this be? She'd heard most of the racing route varied from flat to gently rolling hills. How could a champion cyclist wipe out—hitting a tree, no less—on a course like that?

She joined the others in bowing their heads. *How do I pray for somebody I can't stand?* Well, she'd read in the Bible about loving your enemies. Love *Trent?* No way. But she asked God to help him anyway. And to help his parents.

"Amen. Trent is in good hands." Jackson gestured toward the road. "Please feel free to continue your ride. Volunteers will man the SAG stations, as planned. And if you're worried about safety, another van has been added to patrol the routes."

His words seemed to bolster the riders' confidence, and most of them, though subdued, took off down the country road.

Jackson turned to Liz. "I'm riding back to make sure everything's covered."

"I'll ride with you." The words escaped her mouth before she could stop them. Liz raised her gaze to his. "Trent's a guest at my inn. His family may need my help."

No hostility marred Jackson's expression. He nodded.

While they talked, Miriam had borrowed a cell phone and spoken to her daughter Grace, who, with her sister, was helping at the fifty-mile SAG stop. The sharp lines in Miriam's forehead had softened. "The girls are fine," she told Liz. "But when I see the next van along the route, I will take it to the halfway point so I can be with them."

How well Liz knew that mom feeling. If only she could stay near Steve too.

She wished she could continue riding with Miriam, but her gut continued to direct her back to the Kappel. Their good-bye side hugs were more fervent than usual.

Liz watched as Miriam rode off. She and Jackson gulped power drinks and mounted their bikes for the return trip. For a while, they cycled in silence.

The lovely morning clashed with the solemnity of their ride, like gears out of sync. How could the clueless sun shine so pleasantly? Even more strange, she and Jackson, ardent members of the anti-Trent club, were speeding back to be of service to him if needed.

They might find they weren't needed at all. Why were they assuming the worst? By nightfall, Trent might well rule as king of the hospital ward, wrapping the prettiest of staff and visiting fans around his little finger.

The mental picture both cheered and annoyed her. She blurted, "Who knows? A few blows to the head might knock some sense into Trent."

Jackson's jaw dropped.

Liz slapped a hand to her forehead. "I'm sorry. That was a crass thing to say."

A grin sneaked to his lips. "I was thinking exactly the same thing." They shared a rueful laugh.

"I sincerely hope he's not hurt badly," Jackson said, "but that winner is such a loser."

Liz rolled her eyes. "Try having him stay at *your* house."

Jackson snorted. He was too decent to say aloud what he was thinking, but she got the idea.

Given Trent's gift for making enemies, she couldn't help wondering if other cyclists had been involved. "Did Chief Houghton say anything about racers who might have forced him off the road? Or a car?"

"No, but I only talked briefly with the chief." Jackson swerved to avoid a pothole. "Hmm. Trent never let the other cyclists forget he was that good. Not surprising someone might try to knock him out of the race. But the chief said Trent was found on the opposite side of the road from where he should have been pedaling."

That *was* strange. If other bicycles—or a car—had been involved, surely they would have pushed Trent from the left lane or behind, sending him off the road to the right. Unless Trent had lost total control, veering across the road to the left.

Liz shifted gears and sped up. *Chill. This was an accident. Sure, everyone wants to kill Trent. That doesn't mean somebody actually did it.*

She didn't say much during the rest of the ride, and neither did Jackson. But unlike their tandem-ride reticence, this felt like the silence of good friends.

As they pulled into the town square, the loud beehive hum of festivalgoers' talk and laughter seemed more restrained than usual. Liz peered down rows of booths as they passed. Fewer attendees, hauling totes of goodies, wandered along the midway.

But they clogged the street leading to the Kappel, the apple tree, and two police cars. They packed every nook and cranny of the area around the start and finish lines.

No smiles. Few words.

Disquieted quiet.

A wild urge seized Liz to hit the brakes, turn her bike around, and pedal as fast as she could, somewhere, anywhere but toward the family, friends, and fans of the cyclists. Anywhere but toward Chief Houghton's stony face.

But her traitor feet took her there. Jackson's did too. He faced the chief and said simply, "Any news?"

"I'm afraid so. Trent Cleveland is dead."

7

Liz had searched the crowd for Trent's parents, but of course, they had left for the hospital where, according to Chief Houghton, the cyclist had been dead on arrival. Her heart ached for them. What a terrible turn of events—to cheer on a strong, young son as a champion, only to lose him a couple of hours later.

She couldn't help wondering if Steve was safe. She promised herself to get in touch with him soon.

Houghton questioned various race officials in his temporary interrogation center under the apple tree. He'd talk to cyclists as they arrived.

Now the grim, weathered chief, speaking with the president of the bicycle association, waved Liz and Jackson over. The sweet fragrance of the old tree's still plentiful fruit wafted into Liz's nostrils. Would the lovely smell always remind her of this tragic day?

Houghton and the mayor agreed to close the festival in Pleasant Creek for the remainder of the day. Jackson and the bicycle association officials decided to scrap the day's races and results, moving them to the following Saturday, the last day of the festival. They called the SAG's top leaders with the news. Jackson accompanied the officials to the finish line, where they hoped to intercept and inform any racers who might not have heard.

Houghton turned to Liz. "I understand Cleveland stayed at your inn. Did you see this coming?"

Liz flinched. "Not really. He seemed healthy, happy, and he anticipated winning this race." She ventured, "Did Trent's parents mention that he was subject to fainting or seizures or anything like that?"

"Already trying to figure things out, aren't you?" A ghost of a smile touched his lips.

Liz half-smiled back. She'd helped Houghton solve a few mysteries before. "I might have seen something important that I didn't realize was significant."

"Maybe you did," Houghton responded. "No, Cleveland didn't have any major medical problems. But I guess there's always a first time. We'll have to wait for the autopsy before we can be certain of anything." He lowered his voice. "Tell me about Cleveland."

The quiet tone nudged at her—how could she talk ill of the dead? But truth was truth. She sighed. "He considered himself a rock star. God's gift to women and the world." Liz told the chief about Kandy, Honey, and Amy Lapp and their respective boyfriends' reactions to Trent. "Whether Kandy knew about Amy, I don't know."

The chief said he'd certainly ask her when she returned.

Liz probed, "You're thinking Trent's death involved foul play?"

"Not thinking anything yet. Still have to talk to a lot of people."

"But Trent was found on the wrong side of the road, right?" Liz persisted. "Does that lessen the possibility someone ran him off the road?"

"Probably. Though nothing's impossible, I guess."

Thirty-odd years of law enforcement made a policeman cautious. Liz wished she could stay at his elbow while he questioned the cyclists. But he made her dismissal clear, and she drifted away from the apple tree while he talked to Officer Dixon about clearing out the crowd.

How would Kandy react to the death of her so-recent ex?

Liz winced again. Though furious with Trent, Kandy obviously had cared for him at one time. Liz's guest might well need support. Jason too, despite his irritation with his roommate. From bits and pieces Liz had gleaned from coffee-hour conversations, the two went back a long way. They reminded her of brothers—permanently annoyed with each other yet bonded.

Liz wandered toward the finish line just as Jason came into view, pedaling furiously, his face contorted in a victorious grin.

He didn't know.

Liz's heart plunged to her heels.

Jason crossed the finish line, hands raised high in the air.

Only scattered cheers greeted him. No relatives or close friends rushed to his side.

Jason dropped from his bike and set it down, breathing heavily. He yanked off his helmet as SAG volunteers brought power drinks and subdued congratulations. "Great ride, man."

Chief Houghton appeared beside Jason, drew him aside to the apple tree, and quietly told the young man about his roommate's death.

Liz moved closer. She thought she had prepared for Jason's shock and grief, but horror ripped his face, and with a strangled cry, he slumped to the ground, sobbing like a child.

Liz found herself rubbing his shoulders the way she would have Steve's, murmuring wordless comfort. She glanced at Chief Houghton, releasing the compassionate but stoic man from consolation duty. He would return to question Jason after the distraught cyclist calmed down. But now, the chief walked to the finish line, no doubt bracing himself to inform and question other cyclists.

What a job. Though the role she found herself playing wasn't a treat either. Jason's quaking shoulders finally quieted. Averting his eyes, he jumped to his feet and retrieved his bike.

Liz barely stopped him from riding off. "Don't leave. The chief needs to talk to you."

He almost snarled, "I don't want to talk to him. I don't want to talk to anybody."

"I know." She touched his arm. "But it's important you do. Trent's parents need to know what happened."

Perhaps Jason had a history with them too, because he halted. Gripping his head, he groaned, "Can he get it over with? I can't take this."

"Don't go. It will only make things worse." She hurried to the chief, who told another officer to cover his post while he talked to Jason. To her surprise, he gestured for Liz to remain.

Probably to soothe Jason if he falls apart.

They sat in camp chairs somebody brought. She monitored Jason's body language, his face whitening as Houghton asked questions.

Jason stared at his hands. Yeah, they'd been roommates. Usually were. Yeah, yeah, Trent had been fine that morning. Nothing unusual.

"Did you see Cleveland during the race?" the chief asked.

Pain peered from Jason's storm-ridden eyes. "Once. I passed him." He swore. "Never passed him before. Should have known . . ."

"About how far had you cycled when you passed him?"

"Around sixty miles."

"Did Cleveland look sick then? Upset? Afraid?"

"Don't know. Didn't laugh at him the way he does me—in case he passed *me* later in the race. I just wanted to pass Trent. For once." Jason slammed his fist on the chair's armrest.

Liz jumped.

Houghton extracted a few more details about the racers' relationship. They'd lived in the same town. They'd been racing together since high school, belonged to the same cycling club. No, Trent had never collapsed like this before.

Jason tensed when the chief asked him about Trent's lifestyle. "I never liked the way he played around." He shrugged. "But I didn't have to like it. Trent challenged me, and I got better when I rode with him." Despite his don't-give-a-care words, Jason's face crumpled again.

Houghton patted him on the shoulder and stood, signaling the interrogation was over.

Should she ask Jason if he wanted company riding back to the inn?

He answered her unspoken question by muttering, "See you," and pushing his bike toward the street.

She understood his need for solitude. Just the same, she'd check on him later.

Liz hovered near the apple tree, hoping to eavesdrop as Houghton talked to the racer who'd found Trent unconscious after the ailing star cyclist called 911. However, as other cyclists sat on the ground nearby, awaiting their interviews, the chief frowned at her and shook his head. Obviously, Houghton wanted to question them as privately as possible. Only her direct connection to Jason—and his unstable emotional state—had earned her the right to hearing his interview. She retreated to the finish line before Dixon approached her to move on.

Liz chafed but she understood. Besides, she wanted to be there for Kandy when she crossed the finish line.

At the end of the race, Kandy pumped as furiously as Jason had. With one look at the young woman's tearstained face, Liz knew Kandy had heard.

"They told me at the fifty-mile point." Kandy gulped tears and a power drink as she nodded at well-wishers and wheeled her bike to a quieter spot in the churchyard. She didn't protest as Liz walked alongside. "I always grab my food bag without stopping, of course, to keep my time low. But they flagged me down and told me about Trent." Streams poured down her cheeks. "They offered to bring me back in a van. But I had to ride after that, as hard as I could. I had to."

Liz hugged Kandy's shoulders. But unlike Jason's grief, Kandy's tears seemed to wash away the searing heat of her emotions. Her sobs abated within minutes. Perhaps because she rode the remainder of the race, she'd had time to process his death. And possibly because she already had distanced Trent from her life.

"Do you know what actually happened?" Kandy searched Liz's face. "Trent was in perfect shape. He drove me crazy, nagging me about taking vitamins every day." Her mouth quivered. "Did he have a heart condition? How could Trent, of all people, just collapse and die?"

"I don't know." Liz bit her lip. "But I know Chief Houghton, who heads our police department. He'll leave no stone unturned to find out what caused Trent's death." No need to mention the autopsy, which might upset Kandy. "Since you knew Trent well, he'll want to talk to you."

"All right." The racer, who had powered into the finish, wilted. "Forgot all about my food bag. Guess I should eat something so I'll make sense." She opened it and nibbled dried fruit.

Houghton allowed Liz to accompany Kandy to her apple-tree interview. How did she know Trent? They'd dated about two months before breaking up yesterday. Enough was enough. No, Kandy hadn't noticed anything unusual the past several days. Trent had been confident he'd win this race hands down. Their breakup hadn't fazed him at all. Kandy grimaced. He'd flirted with the other women racers this morning, trying to get her goat, but she'd expected that. It hurt her but made her glad they were through. She hadn't known, though, that it would be the last time she'd see him alive . . .

As the chief wound down Kandy's session, Liz noticed Jessi and Stephanie finish together. From their grim expressions, they, too, knew about Trent. Stephanie said something to Jessi, and they walked their bikes toward the apple tree.

Liz spoke to the chief. "May I suggest you talk to Jessi Hanover and Stephanie Galt next? They just crossed the finish line."

"Please do," Kandy pleaded. "They knew Trent too. And, well, we need each other right now."

Houghton nodded, and Liz jumped to her feet, waving Jessi and Stephanie toward them. The chief intercepted the young women and quickly asked them basic questions about Trent before releasing all three.

Leaving the apple tree's shade, the trio ignored the curious crowd and joined tan, wiry arms in a long, silent group hug.

As Liz watched them, she prayed that the young women, Jason, Trent's parents, and the entire town would find consolation and healing on this terrible day.

8

The glum, heather-gray Sunday evening sky matched Liz's mood as forty-plus cyclists and townspeople joined Trent's parents at the clock tower for a vespers service honoring their son's memory.

All the Material Girls had braved the weather. As Mary Ann said, "No stranger who suffers loss in our town will feel alone." Jackson, who as mayor had spent considerable time communicating with the media, made time to attend. Liz saw a number of Trent's cycling club buddies, as well as most of the members of Pleasant Creek's club. And women racers. Plenty of them.

Coats kept out the sharp wind, but they couldn't shield everyone from sadness. Participants couldn't keep their candles lit. Liz flinched as gaudy lights and happy screams from the midway only darkened the atmosphere.

She was glad, for the sake of the Clevelands, that the speakers emphasized the positive: Trent's dedication to cycling. Jason couldn't bring himself to eulogize his roommate, so the area leader of the bicycle association, who didn't know Trent personally, lauded his accomplishments. Pastor Brad, from Liz's church, Pleasant Creek Community, told the group that Trent had taught them to recognize the brevity of life and the need for everyone to live daily in the grace of Christ.

Liz wondered why her pastor always inherited these difficult situations. Perhaps because he volunteered for such scenarios. Compassion flowed from his words and his heart.

Few faces around her mirrored the Clevelands' grief. The attendees were respectful, even sad. Jason alone exhibited wan, wordless agony.

Dealing with shock since Trent's death, the other cyclists staying at Liz's inn had ridden their bikes until she begged them to rest. But Jason had barricaded himself in the room he'd shared with Trent.

As she'd promised herself, Liz had checked on Jason often. So had his cyclist friends. She'd heard them trying to persuade him to race again the following Saturday. Perhaps he would consider it.

Kandy hadn't been able to hide her pain, but she had decided to stay for the race. Liz scanned the crowd again, wondering if Trent's ex would show up for his service.

Not so far.

Honey, standing with Pixie and Shine, dabbed her sultry eyes with a tissue throughout the service. She carried a white rose. Had the biker babe truly bonded with Trent during the three days she'd known him?

That's none of my business. But conflict still flooded Liz's inn. Trent's absence didn't resolve the storms he'd caused.

The speakers concluded their remarks. As if on cue, the clock tower's bell chimed a few melancholy bars of music, then the hour's deep, solemn *bongs.*

Now Honey's tears flowed. She laid the white rose on Trent's helmet, which had been placed on a small table with his jersey.

At that moment, Liz noticed Kandy approach the group. Seeing Honey, Kandy clamped her hands together. Her eyes flashed molten silver.

Nordic princess set on fire. The heat of Kandy's gaze nearly melted Liz, who had to look away.

But not before she saw the tiniest of smiles curve Honey's lips.

The next morning after breakfast, Liz picked up a special edition of the *Pleasant Creek News & Views* from the inn's front doorstep. Usually, the weekly appeared only on Fridays.

Her stomach lurched. A grainy Trent Cleveland eyed her from the front page, flashing his signature self-congratulatory grin.

She wouldn't have read the story right away—she already knew far too much about it—except that the headline grabbed her eye: Cyclist's Autopsy Reveals Death Caused by Allergic Reaction.

Peanuts.

Trent had died from eating peanuts?

Only a few months ago, another woman in Pleasant Creek had died because of an allergy—murdered. Had Trent been murdered too?

Throat tightening, Liz skimmed the story, which stuck to bare-bones facts. No mention of peanuts, just that the autopsy had revealed a severe allergic reaction as Trent's cause of death.

The turbulent coffee-hour scene replayed in Liz's mind. Beans searching out Bulldog. The biker feeding him a sandwich. Trent's freaking out as if Bulldog had brought anthrax.

Liz dropped into the chair at her rotunda desk. No wonder Trent had reacted so strongly.

But how had he come into contact with peanuts? Had it happened here at her inn?

Panic seized Liz as she mentally scrolled through the snacks and breakfasts she'd prepared for her current guests. She even reviewed a computer file that recorded all her menus. Of course, she hadn't served peanuts or any kind of nuts after that crazy coffee-hour episode. And she'd avoided having them in her private quarters so no residue would remain on her fingers.

Had Trent been one of those unfortunates who could suffer fatal consequences from brief, even secondary contact with peanuts? How could any inn or hotel prevent that?

Calm down. The article doesn't say that peanuts caused his death. Was he allergic to anything else?

She reviewed the news story describing the race and Trent's collapse. Nothing she didn't already know.

Liz rushed upstairs to help Sarah clean the guest rooms. While she made beds and cleaned bathrooms, the question continued to niggle at her: What really happened?

She felt responsible for her guest, but this ran deeper—a passion for truth. She *had* to know what had happened to Trent. But how?

After finishing her jobs and running a brush through her hair, Liz walked next door to Sweet Everything.

Aha. As she'd anticipated, Chief Houghton sat in a booth at the far end of the bakery, giving one of Naomi's giant cinnamon rolls plenty of attention. When Pleasant Creek wasn't such a pleasant place, he often found his way here.

Liz greeted Naomi at the counter, then lowered her voice. "What kind of mood is the chief in?"

"Nice. He's always nice. But tense. A lot on his mind." Naomi brushed a dark curl from her face and gave Liz a knowing glance. "Stuff you probably want to know, right?"

"Yep." Liz ordered a skinny latte. "From the size of that snack, I imagine he's tangling with a major problem. I'll let him eat in peace. Then I'll wander in his direction."

She perched on a tall bistro chair at a nearby table, greeting townspeople when the bell above the door jangled. She tried not to bug busy Naomi.

When Houghton had finished two-thirds of his roll, Liz sauntered toward his table. "Hi, Chief."

He half grinned, half grimaced. "Well, I kind of expected you. Have a seat."

She tossed the newspaper she'd brought onto the table and sat. "Maybe there's more to Trent's story than meets the eye."

The chief set his fork down and exhaled. "I think so."

Liz suppressed questions that threatened to pop from her mouth.

"Given this whole thing involves your guests, I might need your help." He gulped from his coffee mug and thumped it on the table. "Just received the results from more tests on Cleveland. He was taking steroids."

"Steroids?" *Trent, the Vitamin King?*

"Afraid so." Houghton sighed. "As if his folks haven't experienced enough grief."

The memory of their ravaged faces wrung her heart. "So the steroids killed Trent?"

"Nope. The pathologist said the dosage couldn't have caused Cleveland's death." He let his leathery hands drop on the table. "Still, it's a shame something like that has to come out. I'm not making it known, but somebody will."

They'd probably see it on the evening news. Trent's parents would suffer a second devastating shock. Picturing their pain, Liz closed her eyes. Had Trent taken steroids all along? She thought athletes were tested for illegal substances.

However, the cyclist had died from a different cause. She yanked her mind from steroids and turned back to the original problem. "The paper says Trent suffered a fatal allergic reaction. Did that involve peanuts?"

"Yes." His sharp gaze riveted to hers. "He told you about that?"

Liz nodded, then informed Houghton about Beans and his peanut butter sandwich during coffee hour. "After that happened, I restricted the presence of nuts at the inn."

"I'm sure you did." His tone held no accusation. "Just so you sleep tonight, I'll tell you something else the doc said: Reactions this severe occur quickly, usually within minutes after contact with the allergen. There's no way any food Cleveland ate at your inn contributed to his death."

Her misgivings, still stabbing at a corner of her mind, collapsed in a *whew!* But Liz said slowly, "Then maybe he ate something at the SAG station."

"His own granola bars. According to his parents, he designed his own special snacks and always packed them in his personal food bag."

She stared. "But—"

"He'd never take bars containing peanuts? Of course he wouldn't." The chief's grim expression froze her very breath. "We examined the entire contents of Cleveland's food bag. No peanuts or peanut butter. No steroids, either, by the way. But someone had stuck something long and thin—a straw or a needle, maybe—into his granola bars, infusing their centers with unrefined peanut oil."

9

Yesterday Liz had suggested Chief Houghton come over after her guests had eaten breakfast. This lovely Tuesday morning, they would learn Trent had been murdered.

She racked her brains as she opened cabinets and rattled pans in her kitchen. What should she fix for breakfast?

Her intended menu, cheesy sausage casserole, sunshine citrus fruit salad, and pick-me-up espresso muffins, sounded way too cheerful. However, a B&B owner couldn't really resort to serving Dickens-style porridge and water. Liz stayed with the plan, but unlike her usual custom, she kept the names of her dishes to herself.

Her guests dragged downstairs as if hungover. Some probably were.

With platefuls of hot food and steaming coffee, they revived to the point of speaking. Even Jason looked a bit less morose. At least he was eating.

So far, no one had mentioned leaving. Liz tried not to focus on the financial problems a group exodus would cause.

Fortunately, the atmosphere was lightening with each cup of coffee. Now a few wisecracks flew around. Bulldog and Scooby imitated each other riding their hogs, and grins brightened the dining room.

Smiles died, though, with her guests' first glimpse of the police chief. Jason choked on a piece of muffin until Jessi pounded him on the back.

"Sorry to interrupt your morning," Houghton said courteously. "You are close to finishing your meal, I hope. Wouldn't want you to miss any part of Miss Eckardt's delicious breakfast."

They nodded or stared at him. No one picked up a fork again.

"Good. I need to talk with all of you about Trent Cleveland, especially those who were close to him."

An undisguised *huff* from Big Berky.

Not smart. Liz sent a warning glance his way.

Honey rolled her eyes.

"We told you everything Saturday," Kandy protested. No Nordic princess today. Just a weary young woman with dark circles under her eyes.

"We barely knew the guy," Scooby said.

The other bikers nodded.

"I understand. But I really could use your help—all of you." The chief employed his best we're-in-this-together voice.

It was working. They rose from the table.

Houghton had addressed her guests before when crimes had occurred in Pleasant Creek. When she'd moved from Boston, Liz hadn't anticipated this sort of briefing would become a familiar drill at her rural inn.

Liz bustled around, trying to inject a little normalcy into the gathering. "Feel free to take drinks and muffins into the sitting room."

She'd had to fiddle with the fireplace dampers again—she better talk to Uncle Amos, her mother's older brother, soon about fixing them—but she'd managed to start a fire. Her guests, basking in its crackling warmth, appeared a little less tense.

Houghton quietly told them the results of the autopsy, including the presence of nonfatal steroids and Trent's stomach contents that included granola laced with raw peanut oil—granola that matched Trent's homemade bars.

Jaws dropped. Eyes widened.

But within seconds, their reactions changed.

Kandy's face reddened, then paled. She picked at her cuticles.

Big Berky's forehead flushed nearly purple. Was he clenching his teeth under all that facial hair?

An odd glint flickered in Jason's blank eyes, then sparked.

Not anger. Relief? Liz pulled her own stare away from the young man's face to survey the rest of the group. Still stunned.

Anger hardened the soft curves of Honey's face. She spat, "So you're saying someone tampered with Trent's food bag? Someone who wanted him dead?" She speared both Kandy and Berky with a smoldering glare.

"Perhaps." Houghton riveted her with his calm scrutiny. "I would like to think this was a terrible accident, maybe a mix-up as to who got what bag. But according to Cleveland's parents, he made custom supplies for races and packed his own bags, marked with his unique logo." The chief held one up. Somehow, its silver lightning bolt over a star seemed pathetic rather than powerful. "Pretty unmistakable, to my way of thinking."

To Liz's surprise, Jason spoke with his earlier self-confidence. "No one could have mistaken Trent's bag for theirs. And the SAG people at the halfway point wouldn't have screwed it up. The volunteers who hold out food bags for racers are the most experienced."

"Yeah, they'd worked past races. They knew Trent and his reputation," Stephanie agreed. "None of them would dare hand him the wrong bag."

I can believe that. Liz bit her lip. Trent had been nothing if not memorable.

The chief pulled out his smartphone to take notes. "Did any of you cyclists stop anytime during the race? Perhaps at the halfway point?"

Jason shook his head vehemently. "A racer only does that when he's in trouble. I slowed slightly and grabbed my bag from Ruth and pedaled to the finish." He turned to Liz. "Hey, I found out she's your aunt. She works that stop every year. Nice lady. Does a good job too."

Houghton addressed the women racers. "How about you?"

"We stopped at the halfway point," Jessi said, "but only because they flagged us down to tell us about Trent's collapse."

Kandy and Stephanie nodded.

"Maybe this was a prank gone wrong." Houghton's gaze swept the room. "I understand Cleveland sometimes rubbed people the wrong way. Perhaps someone thought the peanut oil would only make him sick. Sick enough that he couldn't finish the race."

Liz closed her eyes, not wanting to remember Jason's triumphant, futile finish. She stole a sideways glance at the cyclist, then realized others were looking his way as well.

Jason stared back. No glint in his eye now. "Sure, I wanted to win. But you all know Trent's beaten me a gazillion times. Surprised me out of my socks when he didn't do it again." He transferred his unblinking gaze to the chief. "I did *not* mess with Trent's bag. We packed ours at the same time the day before the race. He wanted to take his to the SAG tent that minute. I wanted to wait until later when Steph, Jessi, and I were going to the festival. Trent left, and he didn't return until coffee hour." His chin dipped. "Now I wish I'd gone with him." His voice trembled.

Liz wanted to hug Jason but thought twice about it. Thank goodness, Jessi supplied the comfort he needed.

Houghton was tapping rapidly on his phone. "So that's how the bags go to the halfway stop?"

"Yeah, riders eat the food provided at the stops. But most racers bring their own, and we had to take our bags there by seven thirty the morning of the race," Kandy answered. "The SAG van transfers them to the stop."

The chief glanced up from his phone. "Could you bring them to the tent anytime before then?"

Jessi shrugged. "Sure. If you've packed fruit or something perishable, you might wait until the morning of the race. But most of us eat the fresh stuff provided while we're waiting for the race to start."

"I stick to nonperishables during the race itself," Stephanie said, "and so did Trent. Less trouble. And, like you said, he made his own bars and stuff."

Berky drummed his fingers on the sofa's armrest.

Ignoring him, the chief continued, "Was someone stationed at the tent at all times?"

The cyclists exchanged glances.

Kandy spoke. "People come and go constantly, some to work, some just to hang out with other cyclists. Usually a volunteer or two sells T-shirts, water bottles, and other souvenirs. We've all contributed a few hours to help make a little money for the association. But it's not like being a store clerk. If somebody locks up the cash, then grabs lunch somewhere, it's no big deal."

The others nodded.

So anyone could have watched for a chance to alter Trent's food. But who would want to kill him? Liz paused. *I should rephrase that. Who would* most *want to kill him?*

Kandy? Berky? Liz's small headache was morphing into a monster. Did anyone actually like Trent?

Berky interrupted her migraine reverie. "Look, I know you have to ask them"—he gestured toward the cyclists—"all this stuff about Cleveland and bicycles and food bags. But we're bikers, not cyclists. We never met this guy until we came to town for the Hog Wild Ride. Do we really need to be here?"

Houghton said smoothly, "I think we've covered general information, but since all of you have interacted with Cleveland the past several days, I'll need to talk to each of you individually. How about you first, Mr.—?"

"Parker."

Houghton swiped his phone. "Is that your first name?"

"No, it's Sherwood." He scowled, as if daring anyone to comment. They didn't. He muttered, "I like to be called by my biker handle, Big Berky."

"Sure, Big Berky." The chief turned to Liz. "Is there someplace—?"

She pointed. "The library would work." He'd questioned guests before in Liz's quarters, but with the past busy, bizarre week, she could hardly wade through its clutter.

But she forgot about the mess as she watched Big Berky trail Houghton like a hulking bear on an invisible chain. Apparently, the sight unnerved the others as well. They'd witnessed the biker's hatred for the cycling star who had stolen his girlfriend. Now Big Berky wasn't being questioned as a mere bystander but as a possible suspect in his murder.

Liz buzzed around, offering hot cider and trying to set everyone at ease, but they fiddled with their phones, mutely awaiting their turns.

Twenty minutes later, Berky stalked past the sitting room's open door and left through the foyer. Houghton called in Honey.

Kandy pointedly ignored the biker babe's undulating figure as she left, but for the first time since Houghton had arrived, the woman cyclist appeared more composed.

Liz figured the chief would see Kandy as the most likely suspect. Not only had she quarreled bitterly with Trent, but she'd had access to the cyclist's possessions. She also knew more about the SAG tent and how to gain access to food bags.

But Liz didn't buy it.

If Kandy had remained under Trent's thumb, Liz could have pictured her murdering the egotistical cycling star to free herself. But Kandy, though upset, had declared her independence and decided to race, regardless of Trent. Healthy reactions.

Would a woman that strong ruin her life by taking revenge on a jerk ex-boyfriend?

Seeing Kandy's laser eyes illuminate again as they followed Honey's exit through the rotunda, Liz hoped Kandy wouldn't murder the woman who had lured Trent away.

After Houghton called Bulldog into the library, Kandy finally broke the silence surrounding her precarious position. She glanced from Liz to the bikers, then to her cyclist friends. "Look, I know you saw me break up with Trent. Yes, I was mad. Who wouldn't be? But I didn't kill him."

Liz and the others murmured assent, though she wasn't sure they all meant it.

"The whole thing is totally bizarre." Kandy shook her head as if dazed. "Peanut oil! What a weird way to dispose of someone. Or a really risky, dangerous way to stop him from racing. And steroids? Trent wouldn't have touched the things—not only would they ruin his racing career, but steroids would have damaged his perfect body. Trent was a health nut."

"You're right." Jessi exchanged glances with Stephanie. "That doesn't make sense."

At that moment, Houghton dismissed Bulldog and called for Kandy. Everyone tensed.

She stood, then faced Liz. "May I talk to you later? Maybe take you out to lunch?"

"Um, how about supper?" Liz suggested. She and Caitlyn were going for a bike ride and picnic soon. "So you can escape for a while," Caitlyn had said.

Kandy nodded. "Great. Meet you here around five?"

"Sure." In reality, Liz felt like biking to Chicago and staying there. But she summoned a smile and said, "I'll look forward to it."

The young woman's grateful expression rewarded her. Kandy straightened her shoulders and marched to the library. A little later when she finished, Liz caught a glimpse of Kandy's long braid as she hurried through the rotunda to the front door.

After the chief's short interviews with Shine and Scooby, Caitlyn showed up at the back door. "Sorry I'm a little early."

Liz hugged her. "Hey, you can help me entertain the troops while they're waiting."

"I don't know the first thing about motorcycles." The tiniest wrinkle in Caitlyn's nose revealed her mistrust of their safety.

"No problem. I think the ones still waiting are all cyclists."

Caitlyn's early arrival turned out to be a godsend. Liz had exhausted her supply of chitchat. Houghton questioned Pixie, and Jason, Stephanie, and Jessi welcomed Caitlyn, their fellow racer, with open arms. Soon they were exchanging stories and cycling tips.

Liz even untethered herself from the sitting room and helped Sarah clean a bedroom or two. When she returned to the sitting room, she found Jessi and Jason had been questioned, and Stephanie, the last interviewee, had just entered the library for her session.

Jessi wanted to wait for Stephanie so they could hit the pottery booths. But why had Jason lingered?

He didn't show any signs of leaving. Even when Stephanie emerged and the two women headed for the festival, credit cards polished and ready to do battle, Jason remained.

A few clouds grayed the serene china-blue sky, and Liz feared her cycling plans with Caitlyn would dissolve in a chilly afternoon shower.

She *needed* this getaway bike ride. Reluctantly summoning another smile, Liz said, "We'd better take off on our ride, Caitlyn, or the weather may keep us inside."

"Maybe I could join you." Jason's coaxing resembled that of a wistful ten-year-old. Way too cute.

"You want to ride at tricycle speed?" Liz kidded. *Please, God, not today. Send him to Chicago. Or Canada.*

Immediately, her conscience reminded her that Jason had just lost his closest riding buddy. Jerk or not, Trent had left a big hole in Jason's life and in his days here at the festival.

Liz cast a glance at Caitlyn. She looked happy. And hopeful.

"Actually, I brought extra sandwiches," Caitlyn said, "and more slices of my butter cake than we'll ever eat."

Liz didn't mention that Caitlyn's cakes surpassed Mary Ann's and Opal's.

Between Caitlyn's extra dessert supply and her pert, cupid-bow smile, Jason was already drooling.

Liz mustered every shred of kindness she could. "Well, if you two don't mind dawdling along with an old lady—"

"You are definitely *not* an old lady."

Okay, Jason's appreciative comment and charming smile rated a *little* compensation for his tagging along.

The clouds skittered away, and their ride in the country eased Liz's raw nerves. Later, as they basked in the gorgeous autumn view from a hill on her grandfather's farm and snarfed down Caitlyn's goodies, Liz had to admit the afternoon had gone well. Though she felt like the tagalong—did a threesome, besides the Three Musketeers, ever work?—the fresh air and exercise did wonders for a sad, weary innkeeper. The butter cake didn't hurt either.

The conversation was fun and lively and sometimes medical, as Caitlyn, a nurse, and Jason, who'd once worked as a pharmacy tech in a hospital, found more common ground.

He mentioned that he'd decided to remain to compete in the rescheduled race, a move Liz considered a healthy one.

"I'd planned to stay the whole week anyway." Jason munched his third slice of cake. "Besides, that policeman said he was asking people who were close to Trent to stick around awhile if possible."

Houghton considered Jason a person of interest in the case? Liz understood the chief's reasons, but this all-American boy, who'd endured so much from his roommate, didn't seem a likely suspect.

She was glad to hear that while Honey and Scooby had decided to join another biker group at their hotel in Marion, Berky, Bulldog, Shine, and Pixie seemed inclined to stay.

"They'd already planned time off work," Jason said, "and what with Honey's breakup with Berky, I think the others want to hang out with him."

By the time they returned to the Olde Mansion Inn, Liz assumed another bicycle date—one without her—was imminent. Saying a quick good-bye, she used coffee-hour prep as a reason to avoid the "two's company, three's a crowd" scenario.

While arranging oatmeal cookies and snickerdoodles on a platter, a twinge of unease prodded her at the thought of the twosome spending more time together. Why? What could be more natural than chemistry between people who had so much in common?

Besides, Caitlyn was more than capable of taking care of herself. And from the beginning, Jason had been the most personable of her guests.

Wait a minute. Not quite true.

He'd been pleasant at first, but Trent's death had devastated him to the point Liz had worried about him.

Yet today, it was as if he'd changed personalities.

Caitlyn was a lively young woman who could charm a taciturn guy into more smiles, but depression and grief like Jason's didn't disappear with one bicycle ride.

Unless he'd faked it all.

Liz nearly dropped her cookie platter.

If he had feigned that entire display of anguish, Jason Brummett was the best actor she'd ever seen.

10

Well, this was a first.

Usually *somebody* showed up for coffee hour. Or told Liz beforehand if they wouldn't be coming. But a total no-show? Perhaps this morning's interrogations had proved more than enough "togetherness" for everyone.

Toasting her toes by the sitting-room fireplace, she reached for another cookie, then mentally slapped her hand. After Caitlyn's butter cake this afternoon and with a visit to the festival this evening, she certainly didn't need snickerdoodles.

Liz popped the cookies into the freezer—except for a few she reserved for Kandy.

When Kandy arrived for their supper date, her eyes lit up at the sight of the treats. "Thanks, I'm starved! I meant to make coffee hour, but my practice ride took longer than I expected. And after a hundred miles, I needed a shower."

"A hundred! I think you've earned those cookies." Liz banked the fire. "Do you feel like walking at the festival?"

"Oh, sure. Nothing like snickerdoodles to bring a rider back to life." For a moment, Kandy's slightly freckled face crinkled in a little-girl grin. "Where would you like to eat?"

"I don't need much fried food this evening. But I know of one booth with the best barbecue chicken sandwiches in the world."

"Sounds wonderful."

As they strolled through rows of booths, Liz almost forgot Kandy had wanted to discuss something with her. Wood smoke, spicy potpourris for sale, and, of course, the delectable dinner fragrances—Liz forced herself to walk past the tenderloin tent—combined to produce an aroma unmatched anywhere.

They stopped at a jewelry booth to try on earrings and exclaimed over stained glass art at another. Liz bought a set of transoms for windows in her private quarters. Since the inn was close, the artist offered to deliver them after supper.

Occasionally, though, a glance from a passerby or a worker in a booth found Liz and Kandy and fastened on her guest—an unfriendly look Liz rarely saw in Pleasant Creek. What rumors had the town's grapevine spread about Kandy? Wasn't she innocent until proven guilty?

Liz led the way to the barbecue chicken stand, where Kandy bought sandwiches and a big carton of fried mushrooms.

She offered them to Liz. "Calories don't count if we share."

Well, since you put it that way . . . Liz savored several of the golden-brown, crispy nuggets.

Thrusting long legs under a weathered picnic table, Kandy devoured her meal, concurring with Liz's opinion. "Thanks for coming with me this evening." She glanced around. "Not everybody's as friendly as you are."

So Kandy had sensed the silent jabs. Liz shrugged. "Oh, things will settle as the truth comes out."

"I hope you're right." Kandy's chin dropped. "Race or no race, I wish I could pack my stuff and leave this minute. Berky told me he'd leave too. But Chief Houghton asked both of us to stay for the rest of the festival."

He considered them, as well as Jason, possible suspects, then. With effort, Liz smoothed anxiety from her voice. "The chief will work day and night to find Trent's killer."

"You believe me?" Kandy's voice trilled notes of joy and uncertainty. "I—" Her voice died.

Liz followed her gaze and caught her breath. Doll-like Amy Lapp watched them, unblinking, from her booth across the walkway. She was the picture of Amish propriety, and her expression had been boiled as clean as a Monday morning's wash. But did it hide the darkest hatred?

"She's one of Trent's girls." Kandy's muffled voice trembled. "Amish or not, she has to be." Her shoulders slumped, but she stood quickly, tripping over the table's bench. "I-I'm sorry, Liz. I think I'll go back to the inn now."

Before Liz could say anything, Kandy was gone.

The remaining bites of Liz's chicken sandwich didn't taste so good. She finished and left to make room for the multitude of diners at the festival. And to escape Amy, whose stare still found Liz as she ate.

Of course, Nathan must have told Amy he had nothing to do with Trent's death. Maybe he had even said Kandy killed him. But Nathan probably had some explaining to do. When she saw the chief again, she'd ask him if Nathan had an alibi.

The bright lights of the midway beckoned, and the night was unusually warm for October. Liz didn't want to go home. Work and more work awaited her.

But wander the festival by herself? Not an option, especially since it made her miss Jackson. He'd probably found someone else to accompany him. She'd probably run into them . . .

Liz speed-dialed Naomi.

"I'm so glad you called." Her friend's voice struck a warm chord in Liz. "With everything going on, Mary Ann wasn't sure you'd want to come to the festival tonight. At seven, the Material Girls are meeting at the show rings for the Celebrity Goat Obstacle Run."

"The what?"

Naomi giggled. "The Celebrity Goat Obstacle Run. You didn't see it last year?"

"I think I was, uh, busy." Liz had never heard of it.

"Well, you can't miss the run this year. I won't even try to describe it. Just come."

Okay. Whatever it was, it had to beat watching a movie alone. She hoped.

With her hour of unplanned leisure, she searched for the SAG tent. Finding a festival map online, she inched through hundreds of attendees tramping the aisles, occasionally locating a linebacker-sized guy to follow as crowds parted before him.

Near the end of an aisle, she saw a large blue-and-white tent with a prominent bicycle logo on its sign. A few clumps of cyclists, some wearing bike shorts and jerseys, hung out inside and around the tent. One manned an untidy display of water bottles, T-shirts, and energy bars.

Liz found a spot nearby where she could sip cider and greet friends who passed. There she could also observe the people and activities surrounding the tent. Groups, including some Amish, ebbed and flowed. The SAG "clerk" freely wandered from his post to join the others, leaving for fifteen minutes before he returned, munching an elephant ear. This scenario certainly fit her cycling guests' description. With ten clubs represented, as well as many individual racers—not to mention a large number of volunteers—anyone could have waited for an opportune moment, tampered with a food bag's contents, and left, undetected.

Nevertheless, Liz stopped at a booth that resembled a miniature barn next door to the SAG tent. The owner, Lowell Hershberger, an elderly Amish man who couldn't for the life of him hide the perpetual twinkles in his eyes, was a friend of her uncle Amos. Lowell and his sons built the cutest sheds she'd ever seen, some featuring porches, pillars, and gingerbread trim. Today Lowell was doing his best to charm her into buying one. "Miss Liz, you need a *Shetta*? I have the perfect one for you."

"Not today," she hedged, then mentioned Trent's death and asked about the goings-on at the SAG tent.

Lowell's eye sparkles disappeared. "I heard about that boy's *Dōt*. So sad. I do not remember seeing anything odd around that tent. The usual." He glanced at Rumschpringe youth, talking and laughing with English cyclists.

With his almost inaudible sigh, Liz knew any efforts to ask about

Nathan Troyer would be met with silence. She wished him a *guta nacht* and meandered through festivalgoers to a booth owned by Maya Morrison, whom she knew from craft fairs where the Material Girls had entered quilts. They'd hit it off from the beginning, and now she hoped her talkative friend's artistic talents included a keen power of observation.

Thirty-something, red-haired Maya raised sheep and knit sweaters and other clothing from their wool. Liz owned one of her ponchos, a gorgeous gray, lavender, and blue garment that kept her warm during the coldest January.

They chatted a few minutes, and Maya shook her head over the tragedy that had plagued the bicycle race. "He was staying at your inn, right?"

"Yes, and everything's been in an uproar," Liz replied. "Did you happen to see anything unusual go on at the SAG tent over there?"

Maya shrugged. "Just people coming and going, yakking about exercise. Not my thing. I get enough exercise chasing after my sheep."

"Anyone you'd recognize?"

Maya laughed. "Sure. Members of your bicycle club. Amish Rumschpringe kids. Even saw your aunt Ruth and uncle Amos there."

"They volunteered for one of the SAG stops. I guess they always do." Liz lowered her voice. "By any chance, do you know Nathan Troyer?"

"The Troyers have raised sheep on their farm for generations. When mine get sick, I ask Nathan's dad, Noah, what to do. Some people don't like him, but we get along okay. What he doesn't know about sheep isn't worth knowing. Nathan's an expert too."

"Have you seen Nathan hanging out at the SAG tent with the Rumschpringe kids?"

"Not with them." A small frown creased Maya's freckled face. "I saw him there only once."

Liz's pulse quickened. "Do you remember what day?"

Maya counted on her fingers. "Friday, I think. Yeah, Friday. Had great sales that day. A lady bought hats and socks for all her sisters, daughters, and grandkids."

The day before the race! Liz tried to plane excitement from her voice. "Nathan wasn't with anyone?"

"No. Stood around by himself outside the tent for a few minutes, looking awkward. No wonder. I know he got baptized recently, he and that pretty little Amy Lapp he's going to marry. But I doubt the bishop will fuss about his checking out the SAG bunch for a few minutes. The next time I glanced over there, Nathan was gone." Maya's smile crinkles morphed into worried crinkles. "Nathan's not in some kind of trouble, is he?"

"No." Liz could say that with honesty. "I just wondered if he had seen something that could pinpoint why Trent Cleveland collapsed during the race." Honesty? Um, sort of.

Relief drifted over Maya's face. "So you're playing Sherlock Holmes again? Well, if Nathan says something, you can bank on it. He's a good boy. I'm glad he's found a sweet girl to share his life with."

Oops. Liz steered their conversation to a colorful scarf she'd targeted as a Christmas present for Naomi, bought it, and tucked it into her purse. She left to canvass a couple of other nearby booth owners, but they'd been too busy the past few days to notice anything, usual or unusual, at the SAG tent.

Time had galloped by, and Liz dashed to the open-air arena, including three show rings surrounded by bleachers, housed under a barnlike roof. Almost every seat was occupied, including several rows of Amish spectators. Liz squinted. She spied Noah and Kezia Troyer but saw no sign of Nathan. Instead, Rose and Mattie Stoltzfus were sitting by the couple. The foursome's presence surprised Liz even more than that of other Amish onlookers.

Noah even smiled as he spoke briefly to Mattie, and all of them looked more relaxed than when Liz had seen them last. She hoped they enjoyed this . . . spectacle.

Scanning the rest of the arena, Liz caught a glimpse of the Material Girls sitting a few rows from the front, but Mary Ann wasn't with them.

Sadie spotted Liz, stood, and whistled between her fingers loud enough to make the dogs in a nearby ring whine and bark. Two sat on their haunches and howled.

"Wooo-hoooo! Get over here, girl!" Never shy, Sadie waved her arms like a ship's signal officer.

Great. Laughter or glares followed Liz, depending on whose child was performing. She ducked her head as she scurried over to the group. *Maybe I should have stuck with watching a movie at home.*

But no. Most of Pleasant Creek, quite a few festival visitors, and certainly the dogs now knew she had come to watch the Celebrity Goat Obstacle Run.

Whatever that was.

11

Liz plopped beside Naomi, still feeling the stares from the crowd.

Sadie's eyes lit up as a new thought occurred to her. "Liz, they should have asked *you* to be a contestant. You're our local celebrity sleuth. Maybe if I ask—"

"No, they shouldn't have." Liz cut her off. "And no, you won't. I've had enough excitement during this festival, and all I want to do is sit here and watch." *Or maybe disappear.*

"Oh, all right." Sadie finally sat down. "Some people are spoilsports." Liz gritted her teeth.

Naomi patted her shoulder. "In a few minutes, everybody will be watching the center ring."

Liz noticed the setup of various ramps, cones, and hoops, including a portable basketball goal.

A basketball goal? For goats?

If real goats actually participated in this event.

"Ladies and gentlemen, boys and girls," boomed an emcee from the center ring, "today we have the most magnificent collection of goats ever seen on the face of the earth. But that's not all. We also have the most magnificent collection of goat trainers who have ever lived. Please welcome them now as we begin with our annual Promote the Goat Parade!"

"Pomp and Circumstance" blared from the loudspeaker as a line of blue-jeaned young handlers expertly led goats of all sizes, colors, and shapes around the ring. The children had dressed their pets to the nines. A number of them wore straw hats and had bandannas tied around their necks, the ends of which they nibbled when their handlers weren't looking. One bearded billy goat, sporting a shabby wool newsboy cap, reminded Liz of Professor Moss, who'd taught her history in college. Several nanny goats wore flower-festooned bonnets, but the belle of the parade flaunted a feathery pink collar and a sparkly bow tilted over one ear. Two darling pygmy goats pulled a little wagon with wooden signs advertising farms that sold goat milk and cheese. Cell phone cameras flashed like paparazzi. The children and animals circled several times, then exited to cheers and applause.

"And now, what we've all been waiting for," roared the emcee, "our local celebrities who have so willingly volunteered for this competition. I give you our first goat obstacle course runner, Mr. Lowell Hershberger, running with Gummy!"

Liz barely kept from laughing out loud. Between Lowell's wispy gray beard and Gummy's wide-brimmed hat, they could have passed for relatives. She hadn't known her shed-building friend as a celebrity, but apparently he was among the Amish group, who shouted their encouragement even louder than the others.

But Gummy did not appear impressed. The goat yanked free from Lowell and dashed toward the exit.

The Amish man headed him off with practiced ease and grabbed the leash. "Come on, Gummy, back to the start. We will complete this course if it's the last thing you do!"

Given the veiled threat, Gummy appeared to reconsider.

Each run was timed. With a "ready, set, *go*," Lowell displayed surprising spryness as he guided the goat over a small ramp, then held a hoop for him to step through. He ran Gummy through a small maze without too much trouble, but when they came to a small stairway to a plywood bridge, Gummy froze, hooves glued to the third and final step.

"Come on, goat!" The old man gave Gummy a light swat on the rump. "Move!"

Gummy did. Backward.

Lowell stood in front of the goat and tugged. The goat backed farther, then suddenly broke loose and charged around Lowell up the steps, over the bridge, and down again. Gummy sent every single cone flying as he sprinted toward the exit, red-faced Lowell on his heels, yelling at the top of his lungs.

The Amish spectators laughed as Liz had never heard before.

Caitlyn drew imaginary numbers in the air. "Gummy, one, and Lowell, zero."

"I don't think that's how it's scored." Opal giggled. "But Gummy thinks so!"

"Thank you, Lowell and Gummy," intoned the emcee, "but I'm afraid we'll have to add a considerable time penalty for not finishing the course together. Perhaps our next contestants will succeed. I give you Police Chief Houghton and George!"

What? Liz nearly swallowed her teeth.

The chief, looking calm and confident, trotted out the goat with the newsboy cap. He kept control of George, guiding the goat through the obstacle course. They looked as if they had practiced these moves extensively. Liz said as much to Sadie.

She snorted. "Sure, the goats practice. With the kid handlers. But *not* with the celebrities." She stared at Liz as if she'd lost her mind. "What would be the fun in that?"

At the little inground pool George was supposed to bridge, the goat suddenly lunged ahead, and Houghton stumbled and plopped face-first into the water.

Maybe you'd better stick to criminals, Chief. Liz was holding her sides when she spotted Jackson waiting in the wings. He held the leash of the goat with pink accessories. As far as Liz could tell, neither he nor she was smiling.

Houghton grinned, though, and the dripping police chief and George finished the course in fine style. Houghton sank three baskets in a row before exiting with his goat to thunderous applause.

Liz still hadn't figured out the connection between humans

shooting baskets and goats, but no one else appeared concerned, so she didn't raise the issue.

A roar of laughter surged over the crowd as the emcee introduced Jackson and Gracie Lou.

"Mayor, they gave you a sissy goat!" shouted a comedian from the top of the bleachers.

Jackson, why didn't you wear pink sequins too? At first, Liz tried to retain a scrap of sympathy for him. However, seeing Jackson struggle with the recalcitrant animal almost made up for their cycling/dog-chasing incident. Gracie Lou balked on the ramp, she balked at the hoops, and she sniffed the bridges as if they contained explosives. But she adored Jackson's shoelaces, chewing them until he finally persuaded her to stop.

Unjustly deprived, Gracie Lou took her revenge in a unique way. The second Jackson turned his back to answer a heckler in the crowd, she butted him flat on his face.

And again at the water pool.

As laughter convulsed the entire arena, including the emcee, bellowing into his microphone, Liz's scrap of sympathy returned. Poor Jackson, his face and always spotless jeans were streaked with mud, his perfect hair wild as if stirred with a spoon. Though he'd once played on a college team, Jackson couldn't seem to shoot a basket to save his life. One of the kid handlers came to his aid and made the final basket.

What some people would do to stay in office.

Gracie Lou even halted at the exit, but the kid handler once more took pity on Jackson and grabbed the goat's tether.

The emcee regained his composure enough to announce, "Now for our last celebrity! Put your hands together for the lady who can do it all, Mrs. Mary Ann Berne and Shoofly Pie."

Liz and the Material Girls leaped to their feet, yelling approval as Mary Ann paraded a brown goat with cream-colored spots into the arena. Before attempting the obstacle course, their friend dropped to her knees and petted the goat.

"Is she talking to that animal?" Opal pressed forward, as if trying to hear.

Naomi grinned. "Probably bribing it with a real shoofly pie."

Whatever Mary Ann said, it worked goat magic. Mary Ann and Shoofly Pie pushed through the obstacle course like Olympic champions, spectators roaring louder as the two breezed through each event. No head butts by Shoofly. No surprise baths for Mary Ann. Just a steady march toward the end of the course.

Liz pointed to the basketball goal. "Can she do that?"

Mary Ann answered with an effortless layup. And another. Finally, she slung a hook shot into the net that brought the crowd to its feet.

For the first time, Shoofly Pie balked a little, especially when well-wishers stormed the arena. But Mary Ann soothed the goat, and he stood still for flashing cameras as she accepted a trophy for their performance.

"Wow, he obeyed your every command," Liz commented when they reached Mary Ann. "What did you say to him?"

Mary Ann shrugged. "I said, 'Mess with me, mister, and you'll end up a seat cover in my van.'"

So much for the Goat Whisperer. Liz laughed with the others, but she didn't doubt her friend spoke the truth. Mary Ann managed customers, politicians, rowdy teens, toddlers—and goats—with a single sweet, steely smile. She could intimidate anyone.

Except Sadie.

"She doesn't scare me." Sadie had read Liz's mind.

Liz knew that. She also understood the odds were small that she herself would end up as a van's seat cover.

Just the same, she decided never to argue with Mary Ann about quilt colors again.

12

"Looking for Jackson?" Naomi threw Liz a teasing smile as they wandered away from Mary Ann and a reporter.

"No, I'm sure he's long gone." Jackson definitely would not linger for a photo op with Gracie Lou. Liz didn't bother to suppress a wicked grin. Their picture probably would appear on the *Pleasant Creek News & Views* front page anyway.

Instead, Liz searched the crowd for Chief Houghton. There he was, chatting with Lowell and several Amish farmers.

When Liz told her friend she wanted to talk with the police chief, Naomi said, "No problem. I don't need to party tonight. Have to be up early to bake apple dumplings. *Lots* of them."

"I'll stop by for one since I didn't make it back for Mary Ann's giant apple pie." Festivalgoers had devoured every last crumb while Liz had been at the Kappel Apple Race.

They said good-bye, and Liz headed for the chief's conversation circle, where the farmers were excusing themselves as well. "Meet you at Lehman's tomorrow," they reminded each other.

Liz had heard James Lehman had fallen ill with cancer. His friends were probably assisting his family with the harvest. How she loved the way people here, Amish or not, helped each other.

How she hated the violence that had invaded her town once again.

"Want to talk to me?" As usual, the chief zeroed in on her intent.

Liz lowered her voice. "I've learned a few details that may or may not be relevant to Trent's death. I thought you should know about them."

Houghton surveyed the crowd that still lingered. "Why don't you meet me at the station?"

Liz nodded. Privacy in Pleasant Creek was a rare commodity, even at the police station. But a discussion at the festival might as well be broadcast over local radio.

She mingled with nighttime attendees as she walked downtown. When she entered the plain brick building, Houghton was already waiting in his cluttered, musty office with her coffee in hand.

"Sorry to make you walk alone, but I thought it was better we weren't seen together in such a public place." He grimaced as he poured his own cup. "Though I imagine most people around here know you work with me on cases."

"It doesn't hurt to be cautious." Liz sipped the heavy-duty brew. "You remember what I told you about seeing Trent with Amy Lapp?"

Houghton's thick, gray brows joined, as if trying to double his brainpower. "So you think Nathan Troyer had something to do with Cleveland's death?"

Liz hesitated. "I don't know. Maya Morrison insisted he couldn't be involved in anything shady, but she saw him hanging around the SAG tent."

"Maya did? Hmm." The chief sipped his coffee.

Houghton kept his finger on the pulse of his town, so she wondered if she was wasting his time and hers. "Did you already know that?"

"No. When I questioned him, Nathan told me he'd been concerned about his fiancée's relationship with Cleveland but he had nothing to do with his death. He didn't go to the Kappel Apple Race at all. Nathan insisted he didn't know Cleveland was allergic to peanuts." The chief drummed his fingers on the desk the way he always did when he was thinking hard. "He also said he was at the festival every day working at his family's booth. Interesting that he didn't mention visiting the SAG tent."

"He may not be the only one keeping secrets." Liz told the chief about Honey's lakeside rendezvous with Trent. "When Big Berky returned, he certainly would have noticed Honey's absence. He might have seen her and Trent together. That would have added major fuel to the fire."

"The guys clashed over her before that?"

She sighed. "Even before Honey became a factor. For Berky and Trent, it was hate at first sight."

He asked, "Did you see Berky the morning of the race?"

"Yes, he ate breakfast with the others before the bikers left for the Hog Wild Ride."

"He could have visited the SAG tent earlier," the chief suggested. "Though he would be hard to miss, even in a disguise."

"Someone would have noticed his presence." She'd yet to see *anything* escape Pleasant Creek's vigilant grapevine.

"Not necessarily." Houghton shrugged. "I talked to most of the booth owners in the SAG tent aisle, yet I didn't know about Nathan. Festival time morphs individuals into a backdrop of people. Big, small, Amish, English, resident, stranger—even Berky could have accessed that tent and Cleveland's bag without anyone giving him a second glance."

"Or giving *her* a second glance." Liz swallowed. "Kandy left the Material Girls' quilting party early, and Honey didn't go out with her friends afterward. If Kandy had gone for a walk around the lake, she would have seen her guy with Honey. And if Kandy didn't know about Trent's allergy before he announced it, she did then."

Houghton must have sensed her hesitancy to implicate Kandy, for he fixed a penetrating gaze on Liz. When she returned it, he said nothing else about Trent's ex-girlfriend. Instead, he warned Liz to be careful, as her help on earlier cases might target her for trouble. His usual dismissal—trite but true. Perhaps she should take the longer, more populated route through the festival back to the inn.

The neon-lit midway still teemed with laughing groups and cozy couples, but many of the craft and business booths had shut down for the night. On impulse, Liz veered toward the SAG tent. Silent and gloomy, it drooped, as if weighed down by the week's events.

What am I doing here? She repressed a small shudder and traced her way back to the midway. A multitude of gaudy, blinking lights lit her path, yet shadows enclosed her. Every carny's toothy grin hid a dark riddle. Shrieks from the Ferris wheel and other rides joined pulsing music to weave threads of her past nightmares into the night.

Liz stopped at a shooting booth, grabbed a gun from the smirking carny, and with deadly aim, nailed three yellow ducks in a row. He handed her a little stuffed spider with crawly legs. It reminded her way too much of her encounter with a real one in her garage.

So much for a sense of power. She'd run screaming then, and she wanted to now.

Instead, she handed it back, turned on her heel, and strode away.

Only to sense she was being followed.

Ridiculous.

Stupid.

Liz gripped the cell phone in her khakis' pocket and removed it. Dead. She'd forgotten to recharge it.

What's my problem? She could see the inn's gabled roof from where she stood—all of three, maybe four, blocks away. Whatever phantoms stalked her, she'd survive, phone or no phone.

Still, Liz quickened her stride until a carny with a voice like a trumpet yelled almost under her nose, "All right, you macho guys, show your lady what you got! Come and ring the bell!"

Heart pounding, she paused to breathe as the silhouette of a big, brawny man stepped out of blackness and seized the enormous hammer. Muscle Man slammed the hammer as if crushing his worst enemy.

Again. Again. Each *clang* embedded itself squarely in Liz's forehead, yet her feet refused to carry her away. They wanted to remain in the semicircle of the booth's bright lights.

In the lights she could identify the sweating, swearing guy when he finally paused and turned.

Big Berky.

He halted. Haunted eyes stared at Liz.

"Hi," she said weakly.

He said nothing.

Liz yanked loose from Berky's gaze and walked away. Was he her stalker? Had he grabbed that hammer to disguise his actions? Or to intimidate her?

As she reached the end of the festival, she pulled her phone from her pocket again, tapped its dead face, and clapped it to her ear.

"Hey!" Liz forced her voice into happy-cell-phone mode. "Maybe we can get together soon . . . Have you been to the festival yet?"

She and her imaginary friend yakked as she entered almost deserted streets.

Heavy but subdued steps sounded on the sidewalk behind her. Big Berky?

Liz chatted on until she unlocked the inn's front door. Inside her quarters, she listened at the dead-bolted door.

Dumb. So what if Berky entered? Like the other guests, he knew the current code to the front door.

Nevertheless, she listened for quite some time until a hot cup of tea and comforting quilts beckoned to her, persuading her to call it a night.

Some night. In her dreams, Trent, wearing a glittering pink jersey, rode Gracie Lou through the inn. Liz and haunted-eyes Berky, riding a tandem, chased them—along with a hundred barking, snarling dogs.

Liz awoke before dawn, drenched in sweat and seized with a craving for peanut butter cookies. She opened her fridge, where she'd earlier banished a container of dough, and plopped balls of it onto a baking sheet. Fifteen minutes later . . . one, two, three, four went down the hatch. She devoured most of them before dressing and cooking breakfast for her guests.

Soon Uncle Amos would arrive to fix her fireplace. If only he could fix her week as well.

"Doesn't look too bad." Liz's gray-haired uncle fiddled with the sitting room fireplace's recalcitrant damper. "May need to be replaced eventually. Right now, just missing a screw or two and needs oiling." He retrieved what he needed from his farm wagon and began repairs.

Liz, wielding a dustrag, hovered nearby, hoping to start a conversation with her kindhearted but taciturn relative. The Troyers lived near Uncle Amos and his family. Perhaps she might extract a tidbit of information about Nathan that Chief Houghton wouldn't know.

But Uncle Amos gave her little opportunity to chat. After repairing the damper, he insisted on checking her other fireplaces. "Cold winter coming," he said.

Liz managed to persuade him to drink a cup of coffee with her before his ride home. She talked about the festival and asked how the Miller booth—run by both her uncle and her aunt Ruth—was doing.

A grunt, with a slightly positive tone.

She discussed her friendly neighbors and asked about his.

Silence. Uncle Amos eyed her, gulped coffee, then surprised her with a stern tone. "The Troyers are good church members. Nathan's a fine boy. Didn't have anything to do with that bicycle racer's dying."

Liz struggled to reply.

Did her uncle chuckle? Liz nearly dropped her mug.

With a minuscule smile still playing around his silver-bearded mouth, Uncle Amos said, "Nathan can't even kill a chicken for

Sunday dinner." With that, he nodded a good-bye and headed for his wagon.

Still openmouthed, Liz watched him loose his horses from a hitching post and start home.

13

How much do I really know about Trent? Even as Liz pondered Uncle Amos's assessment of Nathan, she reproached herself for taking Trent at face value. Solving a murder involved knowing the victim well. She hadn't probed into his background as thoroughly as she had crime targets in other cases.

She helped Sarah tidy rooms, then took her laptop to the many-windowed four-season room. There she could revel in the spicy fragrance of pots of gold, purple, and white chrysanthemums she'd arranged and drink in the autumn glory of the Jaynes Lake landscape. For a moment, the sunshine's carefree dance on the water almost tempted her outside. But she plopped into a rattan rocker and began her online research.

Trent's name seemed synonymous with awards. Not surprisingly, his website and social media pages teemed with photos and videos of him pumping his fist and raising trophies to the sky. Beautiful girls also crowded every corner of Trent's online presence. Kandy appeared merely as his girlfriend du jour. Liz recognized all her cycling guests in a few photos of his bicycle club. He'd posted one picture of his parents. But Trent's social media really did revolve around him.

She delved into newspaper and online articles about him. Trent had been projected to win several major races. And, as he'd crowed at coffee hour, he'd won a contest in which Gulp!, a major sports-drink manufacturer, agreed to sponsor him as a professional racer. Despite Liz's usual flush of annoyance with his egotism, sadness chilled her search. If Trent had survived, perhaps he would have eventually ridden in the world-famous Tour de France. She could picture TV cameras following his every move as Trent, arms raised in a Rocky pose, sprinted toward the finish for the win. She shook her head. He'd probably pictured it too. Hourly.

Frowning, Liz reviewed the articles she'd found. With no hint of steroid use, Trent had won most races by substantial distances. In one of his few community-minded gestures, he'd even publicly condemned the use of illegal substances and joined with Jason in urging young riders to avoid them.

Even when Kandy was angriest with Trent, she'd insisted that he was clean, and his other cyclist friends had confirmed it.

Another detail niggled at Liz. Jason had competed in almost every race Trent had won—often placing second or in the top three or four riders.

Jason had also been a finalist in the Gulp! competition.

But he'd lost to Trent. Again.

After years of playing second, third, and fourth fiddle, Jason surely had grown tired of losing to Trent. And tired of his ego.

Tired enough to murder him?

Liz inhaled sharply. Maybe Jason's patient sidekick persona disguised smoldering resentment.

A picture of the clean-cut, boyish cyclist wafted through her mind. Jason, a killer? Her brain faded the portrait immediately. *Impossible.* Jason had been the only friend plunged into grief at Trent's passing. She'd worried he might sink into severe depression.

Yet within a few days, he'd returned to his cheerful, chatty self.

Liz rubbed her temples, soothing their tightness but not resolving the inconsistencies that harassed her mind.

What else did she know about Jason? As Trent's roommate, he'd had as much access to Trent's belongings as Kandy. More, actually.

And Jason had become very angry when Sarah accidentally interrupted him while he was pouring capsules from a bottle. He'd never displayed irritation toward anything or anyone—even when Trent acted like a brat. Liz stared at the sparkling lake as if it held the answer. Why did that incident cause such a flare-up?

Who knew? Maybe Jason had just been in a bad mood. But his unreasonable anger suggested he was doing something wrong. Did the medicine have something to do with Trent's death?

Trent had died because of an allergic reaction to the tainted granola bars. If Jason had wanted to kill Trent, why would he have bothered sneaking a dose of nonfatal steroids to his superstar roommate?

If that's what Jason had done. Perhaps he had filled Trent's capsules with a peanut product, using granola bars to direct suspicion from himself to an almost infinite pool of suspects.

But according to the pathologist, Trent would have died within minutes of contact with peanuts. Would he have taken pills during the race?

Too confusing. Liz steered her thoughts in a different direction. Maybe the medicine had nothing to do with Trent. Was Jason doping to enhance his own performance and defeat his rival?

Steroids had been found in Trent's system. Would post-race testing have revealed them in Jason's as well, if officials hadn't scrapped the results? Questions exploded in Liz's mind like fireworks. Was Jason pilfering pills from Trent's steroid stash? Or perhaps Jason was Trent's personal supplier and was doling out pills in preparation for the race. The perennial second-place winner had told Caitlyn he'd worked in a pharmacy.

Yet Jason hadn't been associated with steroids any more than Trent had.

What *was* that medication? To whom did it belong?

Back to the theory that Jason was just in a bad mood. Did any of this matter at all?

By now, Liz felt as if the left and right sides of her brain had flipped positions. But one thing was clear: Before she approached Chief Houghton about the incident between Sarah and Jason, she'd have to find out more details about those capsules.

The first step would involve reviewing the scene with Sarah again.

That wouldn't be easy. Her super-conscientious maid, even more reserved than most Amish, would shy away from recalling Jason's wrath.

Maybe she'd ask Sarah to lunch. Somehow Liz would draw her out. She hoped.

———————— ⁓⁓⁓⁓⁓⁓ ————————

The invitation to share lunch with Liz in her private quarters didn't lessen Sarah's angst. Usually a hearty eater, she only nibbled her sandwich and refused dessert. She avoided eye contact with Liz throughout the meal.

Liz pushed her own peanut butter cookies aside. "Sarah, please understand that I am not reprimanding you for entering Jason's room. I simply need to know a little more about the medicine he'd dumped on the dresser."

Sarah's green eyes bored into Liz's. "You think he was doing something illegal?"

Liz returned the gaze. "I'm not sure what to think. He may have been counting his vitamins to see when he'd need to buy more. But if Jason was doing something wrong, we need to tell Chief Houghton."

Her maid sighed. "I know. But I don't want to talk to the police."

It wasn't a surprising reaction and not only because of her Amish background. Before they were married, Sarah's husband, Isaac, had been jailed on a false murder charge.

Liz said, "I understand. But if you could aid the chief in learning the truth about Trent's death, I know you would want to help."

Sarah remained silent. She wrung the edge of her apron.

You wouldn't *want to help?* How very unlike Sarah. "Is there something you haven't told me?" Liz placed her hands on the young woman's shoulders and peered into her downcast face.

At first, Sarah said nothing. Then she spouted, "That man was evil! He acted as if every woman he saw belonged to him."

"Including you?" Liz sizzled inside.

Sarah's eyes narrowed. "He found out very quickly I did not!"

Liz stifled a chuckle as she let her hands drop. *Wish I could have seen that.* Aloud, she said, "I'm sorry Trent acted improperly toward you. If I'd known, I would have asked him to leave."

"There was no harm done. I am sorry to say such things about the dead," Sarah murmured.

"I am too. It seems wrong," Liz agreed. "For his family's sake and to keep a murderer from running loose in our town, Chief Houghton and I want to find out who killed Trent. You might be able to help us."

Reluctantly, she nodded. "But I am not sure I can."

"You can tell me everything you can remember about the medicine and its bottle," Liz urged. "Anything at all."

Sarah shrugged. "They were capsules, plain white. More than a handful? I am not sure. The bottle was white too—bigger than a pill bottle you would buy at a pharmacy. It had a bright blue-and-black label."

Apparently not prescription meds. "You're doing great," Liz encouraged. "Anything else?"

"Two words on the label looked larger than the others. I think one started with a *P* and the other with a *C.*" She exhaled. "That is all I can recall."

"Wonderful." Liz patted her hand. "You have a good eye for detail and an excellent memory. That should give me a good start in my search."

Sarah said nothing, but for the first time, her stiff shoulders relaxed.

"Sure you won't have a cookie?" Liz offered her the biggest one.

"I . . . suppose I will." Sarah ate while Liz updated her on Steve's latest letter. By that time, mellowed by three cookies, Sarah chatted of her family news. She returned to work, focused on hanging wet sheets outside to capture as much fall sunshine as possible. "If that is all right with you. I am not sure they will dry before I leave."

As Liz accompanied her to the utility room, she assured her maid that she would bring in the sheets later if necessary. While Sarah removed them from the big washer and piled them in baskets, Liz folded several towels, which she took upstairs to the room where Jason now stayed alone. They'd already cleaned the room and its adjoining bathroom. Still, a guest could never have too many towels. Liz tapped on the door and, hearing nothing, unlocked the room and entered.

With one ear on "Jason alert," she skittered to the bathroom. She saw typical guy toiletries but no bottle that resembled the one Sarah had described. In fact, no medicines at all. Liz searched the bedroom and closet, and, with pins of guilt jabbing her, she opened drawers and examined their contents.

No bottle.

Had Jason tossed it out since Sarah saw him? If so, Liz could find the bottle in the garbage, as trash day was tomorrow. The bottle might even contain capsules or at least some residue.

Liz quickly changed into her grubbiest clothes and headed to the garage, where she snagged old leather gloves. She slipped behind the inn's outbuildings to an alley and threw open the trash receptacle's heavy lid. Cool nights had minimized the smell of bulging white garbage bags. But did she really want to dig through them?

What if someone spotted her?

She'd think of something. Liz donned her gloves, dived in, and pulled out three bags from the top of the heap. Actually, if Jason had disposed of the bottle/medicine, he had probably done so not long after Sarah saw him. Then those week-old bags in all their gross glory were most likely located at the bottom of the receptacle. *Eww!*

Hoping that he'd tossed it more recently, she opened the bags and plunged in.

Not too bad. But . . . no bottle.

Liz turned her head to gulp fresh air. Something caught her eye: the edges of the sun-kissed sheets, flapping on the other side of the garage. So clean and fresh. So unlike her right now. Probably not dry, though. She needed to remember to bring them in before nightfall—or suffer Sarah's controlled wrath tomorrow.

Sighing, Liz yanked out the next few bags and rummaged through them. *Nada.*

She'd just steeled herself to open the next layer when a dreaded sense of being watched crept over her.

Not like when footsteps trailed her on her way home from the festival.

No, she had the awful feeling—

"Um, hi." Jackson.

Liz, hands buried in garbage, dropped her head. *Of course.* Slowly, she straightened and turned. For once, he was also wearing grubby clothes. The dark splotches on his jeans were probably from the wood stains he used at the furniture store, which smelled of chemicals. But he didn't smell as bad as she did. Liz swallowed. "Uh, hi."

He tilted his head and eyed her. "Can I give you a hand?"

A battery of thoughts bombarded her. Jackson had thoroughly disliked Trent. If she revealed she was digging through this mess for evidence to find his killer, he'd think *she'd* liked Trent. Or that she was entering senility early. "No, no, I'm just looking for a . . . an old letter of my mom's I accidentally threw away."

Bad choice of lies. Liz felt her late mother's steely eyes boring through her.

It also reinforced Jackson's ever-present sense of chivalry. Ignoring her protests, he yanked out more bags and opened one. "Handwritten letter, I assume? What kind of stationery?"

Rifling through a messy bag for an imaginary letter, Jackson would ignore the bottle she sought.

If only she could crawl into a garbage bag. Liz held up a dripping hand. "Stop. I'm not looking for a letter."

He paused. "Okay." His expression said, "So we're doing this for fun?"

"I-I don't know why I said that. Maybe . . . maybe because I don't want to make accusations before I've found evidence to back them." Mostly true.

"You're . . . searching . . . for . . . evidence." Jackson pronounced the words slowly and clearly.

Liz made herself go on. "For a medicine bottle of some kind, labeled with large wording starting with a *P* and a *C*. Possibly a brand name."

Eyebrows lowered, he said, "I assume this has something to do with Trent's death."

"Yes. It might help find his killer." She crossed her arms. "And clear the names of innocent people."

He searched her face, then returned to rummaging through the bag.

What a friend. The forgiving kind. Liz fumbled through her bag again, eyes blurring.

Unless Jackson was entering early senility too . . .

Together they searched bag after bag. They'd nearly reached the bottom layer when two cold, clear thoughts stopped Liz in her tracks. First, Jason might have disposed of the bottle elsewhere. Second, if Jason hadn't gotten rid of it, Houghton had probably seized it along with Trent's other possessions until the murder was solved.

Before burrowing through a receptacle full of reeking garbage—and pulling Jackson into this lovely scenario—she should have asked Houghton about the bottle.

"Now what?" Jackson peered into her face.

Blast again. She should have pretended to continue searching.

But she told him the truth.

Silence.

Liz didn't dare look at him.

Finally, Jackson said, "We may as well finish. Then I have to clean up and go to a town meeting." The weariness in his voice stabbed her.

"Yeah, I probably shouldn't host coffee hour smelling like a landfill." She gulped. "I owe you, Jackson. Big-time."

He didn't respond, other than to grab more bags. Liz did too, hoping against hope they would uncover the bottle. But her intuition whispered that her second hunch about Houghton's seizing it would prove true. She dug through the last wet, stinking mess.

No bottle.

"I'm sorry." She hung her head. "But thank you."

"You're welcome."

Did his voice hold a hint of a chuckle? Liz raised her chin.

Jackson cast her a boyish look. "As far as owing me anything, you don't. But after all this has settled down, would you consider going out with me again? Somewhere with a little different"—he scanned the trash receptacle and its reeking contents—"ambience?"

She giggled, and he joined in her laughter. "Sure," she said. "I'd like that."

They replaced all the bags. Flashing his lady-melting grin, Jackson waved and walked toward his home. Liz headed back to the inn, every cell of her body screaming for a shower.

If their bicycle date had been memorable, this unplanned one had defied imagination.

14

The euphoria from Liz's reconciliatory encounter with Jackson and the ecstasy of cleanliness lasted five minutes into coffee hour.

Liz, comparing festival shopping notes with Jessi and Stephanie, looked up to see Jason enter with Caitlyn. They weren't holding hands, but something in their body language, in the look he gave her as they helped themselves to the beverage bar, tightened Liz's throat.

Still chatting pleasantly, Liz tried to lay plans to edge her fellow Material Girl away from him. She'd ask for Caitlyn's help in the kitchen. Or maybe concoct a detail to discuss about an upcoming quilting event.

But if Liz managed a conversation, what warning would she give to Caitlyn? "Don't go out with Jason—he might be a murderer. Or a druggie. But . . . maybe not"?

When the two sat on the sofa, they became a couple. His arm across her shoulders. Her laugh, addressed only to him.

Any attempt by Liz to privately communicate with Caitlyn would certainly rouse her friend's annoyance. And quite possibly Jason's suspicion—if he'd committed a crime.

Kandy joined them, as did all the other guests but Berky, who'd taken to disappearing after breakfast every morning. Now free to solicit peanut butter treats from Bulldog, Beans pressed his big head adoringly against his idol's knee. Even as Liz worried, she grinned.

The still-subdued coffee hour atmosphere had improved so much since Trent's death.

May as well try to glean a little information. She steered the conversation toward diets and supplements favored by the cyclists.

Jason didn't comment, but the women cyclists recommended a vegetarian diet with various protein shakes.

"I sometimes take Power Cycle vitamins. But never as consistently as Trent did." Kandy's mouth trembled.

Kandy left soon afterward. Liz kicked herself for deliberately broaching the subject. But part of her gave a silent shout of triumph. A brand name beginning with *P* and *C*! The minute coffee hour ended, she'd look up Power Cycle vitamins to see if the label matched Sarah's description.

Alarm shot through her, however, when Jason and Caitlyn rose to leave. He hurried her out the door, stealing any opportunity for Liz to speak with Caitlyn alone. Through the sitting room window, she watched them take off on their bikes, looking young and carefree—and guiltless. But was he?

"Excuse me." Liz left her remaining guests, still chatting, and dashed through the rotunda to the front door.

Sadie, entering with a large package, blocked her way. "Where's the fire?" Staring her straight in the eye, Sadie demanded, "What's wrong?"

Having blurted her suspicions to Jackson, she hadn't wanted to say anything more—except to Caitlyn.

Maybe it was Sadie's motherly gaze that breached the dam holding back Liz's fears. They gushed out before she could stop them.

Was she making sense? At least Sadie appeared to understand one thing: Caitlyn might be in danger.

"Don't you worry, hon." Sadie set the package down beside Beans's vacant rug. "I know the back roads like my driveway. I'll follow and keep an eye on her."

"On Penelope?" Sadie knew the area far better than Liz, but if Sadie's pink Jeep was hardly inconspicuous, her equally pink and much noisier motorcycle would advertise her presence five miles away.

Sadie paused. "Maybe I'll take the van."

A blind person could spot Sew Welcome's gaudy patchwork vehicle. Liz said, "I'll go. Or you can use my car."

"No, mine," said a voice behind her. A set of keys flew over Liz's shoulder.

Sadie caught them with the ease of a shortstop, turned, and vanished. "Your Acura may be dark, but it's too flashy," Mary Ann said. "I doubt Caitlyn would even recognize my old Toyota, since I usually drive the van."

As usual, the woman kept her finger on the pulse of every situation—probably because of her superior gift for eavesdropping.

After Mary Ann steered her to her empty store, Liz attempted to fill in the blanks, but there were none. Mary Ann already knew all. Like Sadie, with any hint of Caitlyn's safety in question, Mary Ann was there to help.

"But I don't get some of this." She eyed Liz as if she were a puzzle. "Didn't Houghton say Trent's cause of death was an allergic reaction to the peanut oil in his granola bars?"

"He died of an allergic reaction to peanuts, but do we know the oil wasn't put into the capsules too? Jason could have used the granola bars as a blind—though I still think they make more sense, given the onset of Trent's symptoms and the timing of his death." Frowning, Liz pushed a stray lock of hair behind her ear. "Trent couldn't have taken capsules containing peanut oil before the race, or his reaction would have occurred then. And he would have had to take at least one doctored capsule during the race."

"How would a murderer ensure that?"

"That is, if he actually meant to murder Trent. Some people don't take severe allergies seriously. Perhaps Jason only meant to make Trent sick. To keep the superstar out of the race so he could win." Liz winced, recalling Jason's triumphant finish, only to have the race scrapped. She gripped her forehead and groaned.

Mary Ann rubbed Liz's shoulder and knotting neck muscles. Her friend sighed. "Jason seems like such a nice boy. I hate to say it, but I agree with you."

"You do?" *I can't even agree with me.*

"We may be jumping the gun, and I hope Sadie doesn't do anything rash. But something odd is going on with Jason. The incident with Sarah seems a bit weird, and his moods have been erratic. Don't let go of that yet."

Mary Ann sounded so reasonable, so confident. Maybe Liz's current state of insanity made sense on some level. Or it might if she could find that bottle.

The bottle.

She'd completely forgotten about it in her anxiety over Caitlyn. She'd also forgotten about coffee hour. But her guests would survive.

Liz pulled her phone from her pocket and searched the Internet for Power Cycle vitamins.

Yes! One of the offerings resembled Sarah's description to a T.

"Is that the medication you mentioned?" Mary Ann was looking over her shoulder.

"I think so. But I need Sarah to confirm it." Liz glanced toward Sew Welcome's door. "Would you go upstairs and grab her for me before she goes home? I should at least check on what's left of coffee hour."

"Sure."

They hurried out into the rotunda. Mary Ann climbed stairs faster than any woman her age should. Liz zipped back to the sitting room, where her guests had just cleaned the last crumbs from the cookie platters.

In the past, she might have felt slightly insulted that they seemed to have forgotten her existence as well. But having lived through the past week's social wars, Liz gave thanks as they ambled past and headed toward downtown. As she waved good-bye, Mary Ann and Sarah descended, the latter's mouth set in a straight line.

Oh no. Had she caught Sarah in one of her stubborn moods?

But her maid nodded decisively when Liz displayed the Power Cycle website on her phone. "Yes, that is the bottle I saw in Mr. Brummett's room." She said little else and scurried out the door.

That's all I need to . . . to do what? Liz ran her fingers mindlessly over her phone. Would Chief Houghton take such a vague tip seriously? She almost hoped he wouldn't. Jason, a criminal? Her mind might consider the possibility, but her heart refused to grasp it.

Mary Ann read her thoughts. "If he has them, the chief may or may not have the capsules tested. That's his decision." She placed her hands on Liz's shoulders and riveted her dark eyes on Liz's face. "But you should call him anyway."

Maybe. Maybe not. Liz said she had other calls to make and escaped to her quarters to phone two future guests. Afterward, she turned on a rerun—the perfect way to block out any mental quandary—and relaxed with a bowl of chicken noodle soup.

Twilight was peering into her window before she remembered the sheets. Sighing, she trudged through the quiet inn—everyone must still be at the festival—grabbed laundry baskets, and walked through the yard toward the garage and the clotheslines. In the semidarkness as she removed pins from the front row of sheets, her irritation vanished. How good they smelled! So chock-full of sunlight, it was a wonder they didn't glow in the dark.

When she took the sheets off the second row of lines, however, she noticed something strange. Big rips nearly sliced the sheets in two, as if someone had slashed them with an extremely sharp blade.

Liz snatched the basket of intact sheets, sprinted for the back porch, and pulled out her cell.

She'd vacillated about calling Chief Houghton earlier.

Now she hit speed dial.

"This is an odd kind of vandalism." The chief, examining some of Liz's favorite sheets in the inn's kitchen, scratched his head. "Over the years, I've gotten complaints of someone stealing sheets off a clothesline but not shredding them up like this."

"With the festival in full swing, I suppose we're bound to attract a few troublemakers." Liz tried to keep her voice calm, though her heart hurt. She'd hunted far and wide at flea markets and estate sales to match some of these lace-edged antiques. From what she'd seen of the damage, most looked beyond repair. If only she'd brought them in earlier.

At least the vandal had left the front row of sheets intact to hide his destruction. She guessed she could be thankful for that.

"This could be random meanness." Houghton seemed to weigh the possibility with one hand. He gestured with the other. "Or it could be someone is ticked off at you again."

Liz shrugged, but she didn't feel nonchalant.

He asked her if any guests had seemed annoyed. She answered no; the bikers and cyclists alike seemed to like her inn. Privately, she couldn't imagine Jason knew about her snooping in his room. And if he'd seen Sadie tailing him and Caitlyn, he would have retaliated against Sew Welcome, not the inn.

All this crossed her mind while Houghton inquired about other routine matters—whether neighbors had grievances against her and so forth.

"I have to ask you these questions." His shrewd eyes searched hers. "But we both know that someone doesn't like your poking around for clues in the Trent Cleveland case."

Liz sighed. "It wouldn't be the first time."

"Probably not the last, either, because you don't quit." His look held half frustration, half admiration. "I won't bother telling you to back off. Just be sure to let me know—"

"As a matter of fact, I was thinking of calling you." She didn't tell him about Jackson's and her foray into the trash. But she related her suspicions about the bottle of vitamins and asked if he had them.

"Sure do. I suppose it wouldn't hurt to check out those capsules." Houghton promised to have them analyzed. He said the police would keep an eye on the inn during the rest of the festival. His voice gentled. "This wasn't what you needed. I know you won't be alone tonight—your inn's full. Still, you might ask Mary Ann or Sadie to stay with you."

Good idea. Sometimes friends could salvage a day when nothing else could.

Besides, she wanted to hear Sadie's report on tailing Jason and Caitlyn.

Liz called her, and soon after the chief's car left the parking lot, both Sadie and Mary Ann pulled up in Sadie's Jeep.

———

Her friends' righteous wrath as they beheld the mutilated linens did Liz good. Both fussed over her safety until she began to have second thoughts about either staying the night. But cups of hot cider together in the four-season room helped soothe some of the tensions of the day.

"Glad Caitlyn and Jason were riding bicycles most of the time," Sadie told Liz and Mary Ann. "Otherwise, I might have had to watch more cuddle-and-kiss scenes than I did—at least, if Jason had had his way. That boy is gone on Caitlyn. But she kept a handle on things, and he behaved himself pretty well. Didn't have to pull Mary Ann's gun on him."

Liz choked. That Sadie would keep her rifle handy seemed to fit her impulsive, irascible persona. But Mary Ann?

Well, she did keep excellent control of all the committees she ran . . .

"They didn't see you, Sadie?" Mary Ann cocked her head.

"Don't think so. I guessed they'd ride along River Road. It's awfully pretty this time of year. I was mostly right." Sadie slurped her cider with an appreciative *mmm.* "The car and I hid behind the Creightons' tumbledown barn, and I kept a lookout later from the Thompsons' tallest deer stand, the one on the hill. I could see fields and roads for miles from there, and Mary Ann keeps a great pair of bird-watching binoculars in her glove compartment."

Liz didn't know whether to shout hurrah or hide. What if the two decided *her* dates needed investigation? At least they adored Jackson. She tried to keep her voice even. "I'm sorry if I sent you on a wild-goose chase. Still, it may have been necessary, especially if the tests on Trent's vitamins turn up something." She bit her lip. "I hated to point the chief toward Jason as a suspect. But if Jason was tampering with them, the chief needs to know." She exhaled. "I didn't think Houghton would listen to me."

"I told you he would." Mary Ann rocked serenely. "For one thing, he trusts your judgment. For another, he leaves no stone unturned in an investigation. When the cause of Trent's death seemed obvious, he didn't bother testing his medications or supplements. But now, knowing what Sarah saw, it makes sense to check out your lead."

"I should have gone to the chief in the first place." Because she didn't, she'd have to burn her yardwork clothes. Jackson probably would have to burn his work clothes too. For a moment, her mind wandered back to how good he looked, even diving into the garbage.

"One thing, Liz." Sadie sounded uncharacteristically serious. "I'm relieved you haven't jumped on Big Berky as a suspect. I know he was crazy mad about Trent's messing with his girlfriend." Her voice cracked with anger. "What he sees in that hussy, I don't know! He still talks about going back to her." She smacked the arms of her chair.

Look out, Honey.

"Berky's a big teddy bear," Sadie continued. "He couldn't kill anybody."

"I'm glad you have some great new biker friends." Liz patted Sadie's arm, though she didn't necessarily buy her friend's loyal stance.

Press the right—actually, the wrong—button, and almost anyone was capable of murder. But she didn't feel like debating that issue with Sadie tonight.

Evidently, Liz had said the right thing, because Sadie smiled and dropped the subject.

When Liz insisted she'd be fine and told her friends Houghton's plan to patrol the inn, Sadie and Mary Ann, worn out by festival excitement, went home.

Though Liz's muscles ached from her trash-hunting adventure, her ping-pong thoughts wouldn't let her think of bedtime yet. Returning to the four-season room, she stared at the lake. She shifted from vantage point to vantage point. After the sheet episode, she really didn't like the idea of walking alone in the dark, but . . .

Finally, she rummaged through her closet for her old baseball bat, zapped her cider in the microwave, grabbed a heavy jacket, and headed for her backyard bench. Though the night had grown chilly and its surrounding lilac bushes were rapidly losing leaves, the bench still seemed like her refuge, one that had always shielded her from the day's complications and encouraged a talk with God. Even if she was clutching a baseball bat.

Liz plopped onto her bench, exhaling maybe 30 percent of her frustrations. Not a bad beginning.

The harvest moon lit the night with a red-gold glow.

This place was so right. This time, this scene—

A huge, hulking shadow invaded the starlight.

Liz gripped her bat.

Big Berky.

She lifted the bat oh so slightly.

"Can I sit with you for a minute?"

"Uh . . . sure." She moved the bat slowly to the side, not loosening her grip.

He dropped onto the bench like a wrecking ball, rattling her teeth. But he kept a proper distance between them.

Liz really should ditch the bat. After all, how many attackers asked permission first?

Berky said, "I'm sorry if I scared you last night. I had to hammer something, smack it good."

She didn't want to recall the wildness in his face. "You did look pretty scary."

"I'm really sorry. It's been a tough week. For you too." His words rumbled through his beard, then thundered as he swore. "If only that stupid cyclist hadn't messed with everything!"

Liz swallowed. Or tried to.

"Sorry. Guess I shouldn't talk bad about a dead guy," Berky muttered. "But Cleveland broke Honey and me up. He grabbed every woman in sight, as if they were apple dumplings made just for him. And he didn't even care about Honey. Not like I do."

His barely controlled rage almost persuaded Liz that he had killed Trent and he was the dark phantom who had followed her home from the festival.

With his brokenness, sympathy tugged at Liz's elbow, insisting he wasn't that guy. She let the bat slip to the ground.

"I was going to ask Honey to marry me right after the Hog Wild Ride." Moonlight outlined Berky's massive, drooping shoulders. "Had the ring, the fancy restaurant, the roses. Even made a down payment on a new bike for her."

Honey, I'm sending Sadie after you. And Mary Ann. Maybe a guided missile or two.

Another part of Liz, however, wanted to shake some sense into the big man. Why lavish his love on a loser?

Instead, she said gently, "I'm so sorry. I wish things were different." *A lot of things.*

"Yeah, thanks." Berky raised his head. "I wanted you to know I didn't do nothing to hurt Cleveland. Not that I didn't think about it a lot. Imagined what it would be like to pound that *cyclist*," he spat, "till he wasn't nothing but a greasy spot on the pavement."

Liz couldn't repress a shudder. Yet his words persuaded her that Berky was telling the truth. If he had killed Trent, he would have smashed him with his fists, enjoying every minute.

He wouldn't have infused peanut oil into his granola bars.

She hadn't seen any evidence that Berky was doing drugs. If so, he might have worked the capsule angle. But how would he have gained access to Trent's?

Liz patted his giant bicep. "I think all of us felt that way at one time or another about Trent. Chief Houghton recognizes that. He's all about fairness, and he won't back down until he finds out the truth."

"I've heard you're the same way."

"I am. I also consider my guests innocent until proven guilty." She held out her hand. "For what it's worth, I'll do whatever I can to support you unless I run across evidence to the contrary."

"Thanks." Boyish relief filled his voice as his big, rough paw carefully surrounded her hand. "I hope you're right about the police in this town. Some of them love to think the worst about bikers." He stood, and Liz's side of the bench dropped two inches. "Think I'll go for a walk around the lake. Don't feel like sleeping yet."

You weren't exactly my Mr. Sandman either. She watched his huge form amble down toward the pier, then disappear as he took the forest path.

Maybe watching the stars, so distant from this crazy place, would calm her nerves. As Liz reveled in the glorious night, the sheet vandalism, the bottle of capsules, even the murder itself seemed to fade into the background. She tried to imagine God speaking a thousand glowing lanterns into existence. Seemingly tiny, these gaseous, glowing worlds dwarfed her baby earth. *How grand you are, God. How unexpected.*

He'd certainly taken her own path in unexpected directions. From Boston to Pleasant Creek, Indiana. From a law career to that of an innkeeper and, of all things, an amateur sleuth. And from her ex-boyfriend Matt Sheridan—her nose wrinkled—to Jackson Cross?

The lovely night seemed to whisper his name softly in her ear, her heart . . .

"Liz?"

"Ahhh!" She jumped a foot.

Jackson held up a hand. "Sorry. Didn't mean to startle you."

"It's all right." Good thing she'd abandoned the baseball bat. Attempting to collect herself, Liz sensed tension in his voice. "Is something wrong?"

"Well . . . yeah." He dropped beside her.

At least Berky had asked permission. Smelly trash bag memories, however, quelled her slight irritation. "What's going on?"

"The bicycle association representatives were at the town meeting." His chin dipped. "Of course, Trent Cleveland's death has turned the spotlight on the organization. Some media accounts have been negative, especially regarding the steroids in his system and possible negligence in the handling of the food bags."

"Inevitable, I suppose." Her legal instincts kicked in, and she sat up straight. "Have Trent's parents threatened to sue the association?"

"Not that I know of." Jackson shook his head. "But with Cleveland's death, the association's definitely taking a PR beating. Plus, even a whisper of the word *steroids*—let alone their presence in the body of a top racer—makes headlines and sends waves of rumors over the Web."

"Not a fun town meeting, I imagine."

"Not at all. Especially since the association leaders seem to be projecting their misfortune on Pleasant Creek." He exhaled. "They're making noises about discontinuing their connection with the Kappel Apple Race."

"Oh no!" she exclaimed, but the news didn't surprise her that much. Current wisdom would dictate that the sooner the association distanced itself from a trouble spot, the better. "Are they making specific demands?"

Jackson nodded. "A waiver of all fees we charge for their participation. Even a strong suggestion that we pay *them* big bucks. Their sponsorship of the race is critical to attracting top entrants. But if other groups hear we conceded to them, they'll demand similar treatment."

"The festival will go down the tubes." Liz couldn't picture the possibility. "Terrible for the town."

"Devastating, actually. Pleasant Creek depends heavily on tourist dollars." Jackson hung his head. "You shouldn't have said you owed me. Otherwise, I wouldn't feel like I could dump on you."

"We all need help sometimes." She patted Jackson's arm, but he didn't seem to notice.

Only seven days ago, Liz and Jackson and the rest of Pleasant Creek had been busily, happily preparing for the Harvest Festival. Now, just as heavy clouds had smothered the jubilee moon, death and dark secrets were attempting to strangle the celebration.

Liz, Jackson, Berky, Kandy, Nathan Troyer, Caitlyn—even Jason—all needed a breakthrough of some kind.

The clouds were blotting out the starlight. She doubted they would release the hostage moon tonight.

Would the capsule test results bring to light some scrap of truth that would brighten their picture?

Sitting in glum silence with Jackson, overlooking the ever-darkening landscape, Liz had no idea.

15

With one look at Sadie the next morning, Liz thought the day could only get better.

Tears were rolling down the never-say-die Material Girl's cheeks. Her shoulders hunched as she dragged herself into Sew Welcome.

"Whatever is the matter, girl?" Mary Ann threw her arms around her partner. "Are your kids all right?"

"They're fine. Other than Sam finding out how to start his dad's motorcycle and riding it to a root beer stand."

Sadie's precocious grandson had inherited a hilarious number of his grandma's quirks. But Liz, seeing her pain, couldn't laugh today.

"Then what?" Mary Ann held Sadie's face between her hands.

Sadie's voice dropped to a ragged whisper. "Caitlyn called me this morning. She saw me following her and Jason."

Liz froze.

Mary Ann demanded, "Did you explain why?"

"Yeah. Didn't make a bit of difference. She was madder than a wet hen. Said she'd never speak to me again."

The bleakness in Sadie's normally spunky eyes made Liz want to bawl too. "I-I'm so sorry," she stuttered. "If I hadn't been so paranoid about Jason, Caitlyn wouldn't be mad at you."

"You were not paranoid, Liz," Mary Ann said crisply, "and, Sadie, you certainly weren't a voyeur. We all care about Caitlyn. And we still have reason to suspect Jason is hiding something."

Even when Mary Ann was wrong, she sounded right. Despite her doubts, Liz's angst lessened. And Sadie, after a goose-honk nose blow, stopped sniffling.

"The chief promised to call me with the capsule test results," Liz told them.

"So let's go about our business until we hear from him." Mary Ann turned to Sadie. "You and I need to refresh the displays before the festival ends."

"Let's do it."

Mary Ann and Sadie headed for the stockroom.

Liz marched off to the kitchen, scrubbing appliances as if preparing for the holidays. When she opened the peanut butter jar to prepare a well-deserved lunchtime sandwich, Beans appeared as if by magic. Sighing, she made one for him first, then slapped extra peanut butter and jelly on her own. She'd just taken a giant bite when her phone rang.

The chief! Her cheeks were so stuffed that she couldn't spit it out to answer. Liz chewed and gulped frantically while Beans, having perfected his peanut-butter-eating technique, swallowed his whole.

She picked up a millisecond before the call went to voice mail. "'Ullo," she choked out.

"Liz?" Houghton's infinitely sane voice vibrated between annoyance and concern. "Are you all right?"

"Yessff." She forced down the last wad of sandwich and managed to clear her throat enough to talk. "I had a mouthful of sandwich. Did you get the test results back?"

"Yep. Steroids. But nothing related to peanuts."

Liz clutched the phone to her ear, wishing she'd been wrong. Totally wrong.

"Looks like somebody added small doses to twenty-one of the capsules—roughly half of those in the bottle. Certainly not enough to poison anybody. But sufficient to get Trent disqualified from our race and future ones." He paused. "Also found fingerprints that weren't Trent's. Is Jason around now?"

"No." Her stomach was tossing the PB&J like a ball. "He usually comes for coffee hour—about four."

"If you see him before then, call me. In the meantime, we'll be looking for him. I should talk to Sarah too. Maybe around three?"

"She's working today. I'll tell her."

"I know you'll keep all this under your hat."

She would, though she ached to reassure Sadie. Her friend's vigilance might well have been rational. Sort of.

On the other hand, Liz tried not to think of Caitlyn's happy face when she was with Jason. And how soon that would end.

Liz hung up and fed the rest of her sandwich to Beans. He licked his chops with doggy ecstasy.

"Right now, I'd love to change places with you, boy." She scratched his ears, dreading coffee hour more than she'd thought possible.

--- ///////////////////////// ---

A thunderstorm had driven her guests from the festival and back to the inn early. No sign of Jason yet, though Berky had arrived and was eating snickerdoodles at an alarming rate. Liz hurried to the kitchen and threw two more pans into the oven.

When the cookies were ready, she slid several onto a plate and took them to the nearby library, where Chief Houghton and Sarah talked. She tapped on the closed door, then quickly slipped inside.

"No sign of Jason." Liz clucked her tongue. "If he doesn't show today at coffee hour, it'll be only the second time since he arrived."

Sarah sat straight in an armchair, refusing to acknowledge the comfy cushions so foreign to the area's Amish homes. Though pale and silent, she accepted the cookies Liz offered.

The chief acknowledged Liz's information with a nod. His eyes lit up at the sight of the treats. Well, why not? Everyone needed a warm cookie sometimes—especially when he might have to arrest a nice young man.

Houghton said, "We're finished here. Sarah can go back to work."

"Or you can go home a little early," Liz suggested.

Relief crossed Sarah's stern face. She hesitated. "If you don't mind."

"Of course not." Liz waved her out the door, then lowered her voice. "This is tough on Sarah," she said to Houghton.

"I know. She's even agreed to testify in court if necessary. Very unusual for an Amish person."

"I'll let you know if and when Jason shows up." If only she could skip coffee hour and grab a break at Naomi's bakery. Or maybe at a café in China.

She made herself plate the remaining snickerdoodles and take them to the sitting room. Her guests' laughter greeted her before she entered. Bulldog had won something at a booth on the midway, and everyone took turns guessing what it was.

"You're the detective." Jessi waved a finger at Liz. "What do you think it is?"

"Um, maybe a . . . furry toilet-paper holder?" Made as much sense as anything else she could think of.

Berky bellowed, "How much did you spend winning that thing, Bulldog?"

"Don't know." Bulldog's head drooped exactly as Beans's did when Liz caught him digging in the flower beds on a rare energetic day.

They all teased the gullible biker but allowed him to take extra cookies in consolation.

Save a couple for Jason. Liz almost said it.

"Hey, save some snickerdoodles for me." Jason said it himself. He stood in the doorway, wearing his charming grin that always generated smiles in return. Caitlyn stood behind him.

Heartsick, Liz offered cookies as others greeted them. Before long, Caitlyn was chatting with Kandy, Jessi, and Stephanie.

Liz texted the chief, then slipped to Jason's side. "I need to talk to you," she said quietly. "Maybe out in the foyer?"

Jason's eyebrows rose, but he followed her out the door. At the sight of Houghton, he halted. No grin now. *Guilty.* His own expression passed judgment on him.

As the chief motioned Jason into the library, Liz fled to the rotunda, then to her quarters.

After composing herself, she headed for the sitting room. She hoped to draw Caitlyn aside before her friend saw the police take Jason downtown.

But no. As Liz approached the group, Caitlyn emerged from the library, her stoic face white against apple-red hair. A dejected Jason—sans handcuffs, thank heaven—followed, Houghton steering him out the front door.

Liz's footsteps echoed as she crossed the foyer to Caitlyn, immobile as a sculpture. She touched her shoulder. "Can I help?"

"Good intentions or not, you still don't have the right to spy on me." Standing at attention in the dusky four-season room, Caitlyn blasted a bullet of a look at Sadie, then shot more at the other Material Girls, who were listening to her rant. She exploded, "I suppose you all were in on this."

"I wasn't." Opal's prim face tightened. "But if I'd been around, I would have done the same thing."

"Not sure I would have agreed," Naomi said, "but I see why Sadie felt the need to tail you." She added gently, "I think you do too, Caitlyn."

"That isn't the point!" Clasping her hands behind her head, she spoke through gritted teeth. "My brothers treat me like a twelve-year-old. But you never have—until now."

Liz tried to think of something helpful to say. But her earlier phone call to Chief Houghton had confirmed Jason's fingerprints on Trent's bottle. Jason had confessed to doping the cycling star's vitamins.

Liz had told Caitlyn everything, but instead of dealing with that devastating news, she'd projected her anger onto them.

"I would have done the same thing for Liz. Or Naomi," Sadie protested. "Or Mary Ann. Not that she'll need it."

"Says who?" her partner deadpanned.

A trickle of laughter greeted their exchange. But Caitlyn's taut face didn't relax one iota.

Liz sought Caitlyn's gaze. "We all need help at times. The Material Girls have saved my life more than once by checking on me. You were part of that." Lowering her voice, she chose her words carefully. "I'm sorry about Jason. I wish things were different."

"So do I," Caitlyn muttered, then lashed out. "We'd only gone out a few times. I thought he might be special—eventually. But there's always *something* that goes wrong." She grabbed her bag and coat. "I'm tired. I don't want to talk about it anymore."

"No leaving without a hug." Mary Ann blocked the door to the inn.

Sadie guarded the door to the backyard.

The others swooped around Caitlyn. She didn't pull away.

The Sew Welcome partners joined them in a group embrace.

When they stepped back, Caitlyn flung at them, "Don't think you've heard the last of this." But the heat in her voice had cooled several degrees. She strode outside and stalked around the inn toward the parking lot.

The Material Girls took a collective breath, then exhaled.

"Men!" Sadie sputtered. "I had a good one, God bless him. But there aren't many of them around these days."

"I don't think Jason's a bad guy. He let his competitive side control him." Liz sank into a chair. "Trent would have made anyone crazy. If only Jason had struck out on his own a long time ago."

"So you don't think Jason doctored the granola bars?" Sadie cocked her head like an inquisitive cockatoo.

"No." Liz thumped her chair's arm. "Why would Jason attempt to disqualify Trent with steroids if he was planning—and it took careful planning—to kill him with the granola bars?"

"It doesn't make sense," Mary Ann agreed.

Besides, he wouldn't kill Trent. Liz felt sure of it. Though feelings certainly did not equal evidence. Many smart people had been fooled by a murderer's clean-cut appearance.

She made up her mind to stop by the police station later to ask Houghton about the details of Jason's confession. Did the chief believe Jason had anything to do with the granola bars?

Right now, she didn't think she could stir from her chair. Having guests arrested drained the energy from an innkeeper.

Opal sat down next to Liz and slipped an arm around her. "We can't live other people's lives for them," she said softly. "Hopefully, this boy has learned a lesson."

"Definitely the hard way." Liz nestled a little longer. Strange how a warm, slightly flabby arm and a faint, flowery fragrance could be so comforting.

"I have no idea what the criminal penalties are for doping," Naomi said, "but if there's no connection between Jason and the granola bars and his past record is clean, we can hope the courts will take that into account." She eyed Liz. "Have you eaten anything today?"

"Too busy for breakfast. But I ate a sandwich for lunch . . ." Actually, she'd fed most of it to Beans. "Um, maybe I didn't. And everything broke loose during coffee hour."

"I didn't think so. Your eyes have that glazed look they always take on when you forget to eat. Just a sec." Naomi left the room.

She returned and handed Liz a sub and a glass of milk. "I wish I could stay and watch you eat every bite, but I have to get back to the bakery."

"And Caitlyn thinks we mother *her* too much." Liz rolled her eyes, but the sandwich tasted so good.

Mary Ann and Sadie, having closed the shop earlier, were headed to the church to help prepare for its huge festival rummage sale the next day. Opal was helping too.

"Don't worry too much about Jason," Mary Ann advised before they exited to the parking lot. "Remember, he did this to himself."

After they departed, Liz savored the quiet. One part of her wanted to crack a window, sit motionless amid velvet darkness, and listen to the last cricket concert of the season. The other part prodded her to visit the police station to find out what had happened to Jason.

Staying here won't keep me from thinking about him. Liz threw on her coat and walked downtown.

16

"It's about time you got here." The chief gave Liz one of his scowl-smiles. "Expected you a lot sooner than this."

"Have to eat sometime." She tried to grin.

He drummed his fingers on his desk, which was even messier than usual. "I suppose you want to hear about Brummett's confession, but first I have to tell you I haven't made much progress in tracking down your sheet vandal. No fingerprints, and so far, I haven't found anyone who saw him."

Liz knew he couldn't question every festivalgoer in Pleasant Creek. "I appreciate your efforts, but I'm more concerned about Jason."

"I figured you were." Houghton leaned back in his chair. "When I told Brummett we'd found two of his fingerprints on Cleveland's vitamin bottle, he could have claimed he'd borrowed some from his roommate. Would have been a decent cover. But the kid's a lousy liar. Told me outright he'd put steroids in Cleveland's capsules because he was tired of losing to him."

Despite Liz's distress, a small flare of satisfaction lifted her spirits. Jason had made a huge mistake, but he wasn't a criminal at heart. "Do you see any connection between him and the granola bars?"

For a moment, the only sound Houghton made was the *thrum-thrum* of his fingertips. "No. At least, not yet."

"What does Jason say about them?"

"He denies having anything to do with Cleveland's food. Says the first he heard about the granola bars was the morning I questioned all your guests when they learned the autopsy results." A glimmer of pity shone in his eye. "Before that, Brummett thought he'd put an overdose in the capsules and had accidentally killed Cleveland."

"Jason was so distraught at first." Liz hated remembering. "No wonder! Now his big mood change makes sense. He was so relieved he didn't kill Trent that he downplayed his responsibility in the doping. Apparently, Jason thought he'd gotten away with it."

"We always think we're smarter than we are. Smarter than everyone else. Especially the police." A grin crept across his weathered face. "Even smarter than the nice lady who fixes us breakfast every morning."

Liz mustered a small smile, but sadness trumped the half-hidden compliment. "The real killer probably thinks he's gotten away with Trent's murder too."

Houghton's grin disappeared. "Any new ideas?"

"If I think of anything, I'll let you know." She thanked him and started to leave.

"One thing." He stood and leaned over his desk. "I'm not saying flat out that Brummett is cleared of murder, okay? But if the real guy finds out Brummett's not a suspect, the killer may feel more vulnerable. Antsy killers are dangerous, especially to people they think may be onto them." He studied her. "Anything else questionable happen lately?"

Liz told him about the dead-cell-phone adventure. "Probably nothing but my own paranoia. I'm getting good at that."

"I've told you and told you to keep your phone charged up." His voice took on dad accents. "And you know my number. Use it."

She promised and left.

The earlier thunderstorm had washed the night air clean. Its freshness revived Liz too. Where to now? Home? Listening to crickets didn't sound satisfying anymore.

Wandering the festival again didn't, either, especially after possibly being followed the last time. But the incredible smells of cinnamon-roasted almonds and apple-something beckoned to her not-quite-full stomach. Perhaps Aunt Ruth was still working at the Miller booth. The point of Liz's flickering inner compass stopped. She wouldn't mind a little more mothering after this tough week. Aunt Ruth was just the person to do it.

Avoiding the aisles where closed booths made crowds sparse, Liz wound her way toward her aunt's area.

She stopped so suddenly that a cowboy-hatted couple behind her nearly ran over her. Murmuring apologies, she reversed her route, glancing toward the couple who had halted her steps.

Nathan Troyer and Amy Lapp. Standing a sheet of paper's thickness apart, they'd sequestered themselves in a small niche between three tents. Liz, while trying not to stare, searched their faces. They looked like they had never heard of Trent Cleveland.

Had she and the chief made too much of Amy's fling with Trent? She hoped so. This Amish prince and princess should live happily ever after. Liz chuckled. Nathan never looked less like a killer than now. He appeared positively moonstruck.

Liz continued to the Miller booth. At first, she spotted only her cousin Phoebe at the counter. But Aunt Ruth's black Kapp bobbed in the background as she inventoried wares.

Phoebe, a few years younger than Liz, gave her a family kind of smile. Unlike most of Liz's other recently discovered Amish relatives, Phoebe had warmed to Liz immediately.

Aunt Ruth drew Liz inside the booth, threw her arms around her in a very un-Amish hug, and told her she needed apple cake right now. "You've been working too hard, I see. When will you learn, *Töchter*?"

"When you do." Her aunt's loving solicitousness made Liz feel like a daughter.

They chatted while Liz devoured an enormous chunk of Aunt Ruth's delicious apple cake with maple glaze.

An angry male voice speaking in the local Swiss dialect from the tent next door, however, gave Liz pause. "He doesn't sound happy."

Phoebe looked uncomfortable. "Reuben Stoltzfus usually isn't."

"Is he related to Rose and Mattie?"

"Their father." Aunt Ruth busily stacked apple cakes in a display. Phoebe permitted herself a slight eye roll. "I am glad Reuben was gone so Rose and Mattie could help at the bicycle race this year. Sometimes he hardly lets them leave the house."

Ruth aimed a pointed look at her daughter.

Hard slaps and muffled shrieks sounded from the back of the Stoltzfus tent. A big man in Amish dress, much larger than most men in his community, stormed out of the booth and strode away.

Aunt Ruth's kind face hardened.

Liz set down her fork. The Amish used corporal punishment in disciplining children. But the cries she'd just heard did not sound like those from a child. "Do Rose and Mattie have younger siblings?"

"No," Phoebe answered. "Reuben often is harsh. He has said before he would rather they had been sons."

Again, that *hush!* look from her mother. Hesitantly, Ruth said, "Reuben's wife died two years ago. I grieved when I lost my Benjamin. It is a hard thing to bear to lose one's spouse."

That does not justify mistreatment. Liz considered accosting the man and giving him a piece of her mind. But would that help his daughters or make their lives worse? Most Amish avoided police intervention, especially in cases of family violence.

Ruth retreated to the tiny back room of the booth to fetch more apple cakes—or to avoid the issue?

Liz asked Phoebe, "Does this happen often?"

"Too often." Phoebe tightened her jaw. "The church elders have spoken to Reuben, but he shows no sign of changing." She sighed. "Rose has not helped matters, I am afraid. These past three or four years, she has refused all marriage possibilities, saying her English man soon will speak to the bishop and seek to be baptized. Now our young men ignore her. Such doings have humiliated Reuben beyond words."

"How sad," Liz said. Inwardly, she burned with indignation. How dare the man abuse his daughters that way? And that scuzzball who had promised Rose the moon—Liz's fingers itched to wring his neck. He sounded like a Trent kind of guy.

Exactly like Trent.

Her stomach twisted.

Could Rose have fallen prey to the egomaniac's charms?

And to a quiet, murderous rage when she finally realized he would never be hers?

While Phoebe waited on several customers, Liz mindlessly puttered and pondered the bizarre scenario. Reserved, sweet-faced Rose, who hardly spoke above a whisper? Who had been steeped in turn-the-other-cheek doctrines since birth?

But then, so had Rose's father . . .

None of Liz's other relatives had breathed a word of the Stoltzfus situation, not even Miriam. Lately, Liz had almost forgotten she was an outsider. Now, with Rose's story, Liz realized how much she didn't know.

If Phoebe, having worked all week next to the Stoltzfus tent, hadn't passed her point of tolerance tonight, Liz might still be in the dark.

Uncle Amos and his wagon arrived with more supplies and wooden items to sell the next day.

Liz greeted him, and as she helped him unload, she mentally listed facts and possibilities. According to Phoebe, Rose's loyalty to this English boyfriend had lasted three or four years. If Trent was in fact this mystery man, Rose had watched him woo numerous women during several festivals, all the while making her promises he never planned to keep.

But Rose had suffered even further. She hadn't been exactly shunned by the Amish community because of loyalty to her English love, but her life had been reduced to a miserable existence with an abusive father, with little prospect for change.

Spurned and trapped? Yes, living like that could motivate a woman to commit murder. The factors that implicated Kandy seemed weak in comparison.

Having known Trent for an extended time, surely Rose would have been aware of his allergy. For Amish women, food was strongly connected to love. While Rose couldn't invite Trent over for Sunday dinner, they probably went on picnics in secluded locations. She no doubt had baked pies, cookies, or other offerings for him, learning to avoid the luscious peanut butter pie and cookies Miriam and many other Amish women made for their families.

Working at her father's booth, Rose had ample opportunity to tamper with Trent's food bag at the SAG tent. As just another Amish volunteer for the Kappel Apple Race, she wouldn't have stood out if she'd visited it.

Or perhaps she'd served at a SAG stop. Rose could not have doctored Trent's bag at any stop but the halfway point, as hundred-mile racers grabbed food only at that location.

Liz didn't recall seeing Rose at the earlier stop, where she and Jackson had turned around. Her heartbeat thudding above the night's carnival noises, she asked, "Phoebe, did Rose work with you and your mother at the Kappel Apple Race?"

"She did."

Behind Liz, Aunt Ruth demanded, "May I ask why that is of interest to you?"

Turning, Liz marveled at how the sharp glance of the small Amish woman so perfectly resembled that of her own late mother.

Phoebe's last customer had left, laden with jars of apple butter. Liz's cousin reddened at the realization she'd said too much, but she aimed a similar steely gaze at Liz.

She'd wanted to keep quiet about her suspicions, as Houghton had advised. But there was no escaping two relatives who, though appearing to live in the nineteenth century, were equipped with X-ray vision.

Liz gestured for them to head to the back room and told them what was on her mind. Uncle Amos, who had appeared preoccupied with his work, joined them. She could almost see his shrewd, orderly mind cataloging the details of her story.

He finally broke his silence. "You believe Rose Stoltzfus might have killed the English racer because he rejected her. That is *vëschta*, very bad."

"I don't necessarily believe it," Liz admitted. "It's only a hunch."

Aunt Ruth's mouth was set in a firm line. "You also want to know if we saw Rose meddle with food bags. For me, the answer is no." Her chin dipped slightly. "But all of us were readying food for the riders, as well as preparing to throw the racers' bags to them. I suppose one of the other helpers could have noticed something amiss."

"I only remember Rose seemed even quieter than usual," Phoebe recalled, frowning, "except for a tiff with her sister. But that did not last long."

"Did she pay particular attention to Trent's arrival? Toss him his bag?"

Ruth shook her head. "I do not know who threw it to him. The bags were numbered, of course, and we checked off a list as to which bag went with which racer. But we were not individually assigned to riders or bags."

"Even if you had been, that doesn't mean the 'tosser' was the poisoner." *Complications. Always, complications.*

"I did not recall Rose's reaction to the English racer." Phoebe shrugged. "We all cheered as he approached because he was the leader."

All three fell silent and stared at Liz in the lantern light. Liz felt as if she stood in a spotlight.

"I guess this is the first time I even considered someone at a SAG stop might have caused Trent's death." Liz chuckled mirthlessly. "He had numerous enemies lurking among his supposed friends, all people with ample motivation to kill him. I'm sure Chief Houghton thought of SAG stop volunteers, but neither of us knew of any reason to suspect one." She exhaled. "Until now."

Silence again.

Amos fixed his gaze on Liz. "This is a serious charge."

She tried not to wilt in the face of their scrutiny. "I know."

He continued relentlessly, "The only reason we listen is because you have pursued justice in the past and uncovered it."

"And because we know your heart." Aunt Ruth patted Liz's shoulder.

Only a brief touch, but it somewhat soothed the fear that her beloved kin would ostracize her. She took a deep breath. "Am I correct that the volunteers at the halfway point were mostly Amish?"

"All were, I believe." Phoebe counted them on her fingers. "Uncle Amos, *Mutter*, and me; Rose and Mattie, who brought the Troyer boys with them; old Abram Schwartz; Enoch Fischer—Miriam's brother, you know—and his family. They brought Miriam's girls with them too."

Quite a bunch. Family togetherness defined everything the Amish did. Liz said, "Then they will avoid answering my questions, especially regarding someone within their community."

Uncle Amos nodded. An almost tangible silent communication crisscrossed between him and Liz's women relatives. Finally, he said, "We will ask around as we can. But such a task may take longer than you imagine." For the first time, a hint of a smile stirred his gray-tinged beard.

"I'll try to be patient." Liz wanted to throw her arms around him but wisely restrained herself. She did hug Ruth and Phoebe.

Uncle Amos would not hear of her walking back to the inn. "Alone? At night?"

She didn't tell him about the sheet vandalism. Or the dead-cell-phone incident. Nor that she'd often ridden the Boston subway at midnight. Instead, she sat meekly beside him on the wagon seat as his big horses ambled to her home.

The next morning, Liz fixed a breakfast of blueberry pancakes, perfect for carb-loading the day before the rescheduled Saturday race. Afterward, Kandy left on her bike, and Liz cornered Stephanie and Jessi in their room. Had they noticed anything unusual at the halfway point of the race?

"Actually, I don't remember anything other than hearing about Trent's collapse," Stephanie said.

"It was a total blur," Jessi agreed. "I cried out of sheer shock."

"Mostly, we tried to be there for Kandy. Talk about shock." Stephanie clucked her tongue. "She was practically catatonic. She turned so white and sat so still, *she* looked dead."

"The volunteers at the halfway point were very caring," Jessi said. "But I didn't notice anything different about them or what they did. They were Amish—you know, wearing those long dresses and caps. The guys wore identical shirts and hats. They all looked alike to me."

"Ditto," Stephanie concurred. "Chief Houghton asked the same thing when he interviewed us. I wasn't much help then either."

So the chief had entertained the possibility that the tampering had taken place at the SAG stop. Funny he hadn't mentioned that.

After the cyclists left, Liz gave herself a talking-to. *I'm not on the police force, right?* Surely, Houghton kept many of his ideas to himself.

Which ones?

Her curiosity continued to drive her crazy as she went about her business. How could everything and everyone—herself included—carry on so normally when a man had been murdered? How long before her relatives uncovered small, "unimportant" factors that could bring his killer to justice?

Or would they discover anything?

As Liz sat at her rotunda desk and fought with her financial accounts, she cast envious glances at Beans. The bulldog, sprawled on his rug, measured the days in naps. He did not fret about his next walk, his next bath, not even his next peanut butter sandwich.

If nothing else, Beans knew how to wait.

But for Liz, it was the hardest thing of all.

17

Liz didn't have to wait long to hear from her relatives.

Miriam, her only cousin who owned a business phone, woke Liz before six on the morning of the race. "Your aunt Ruth was attacked last night, but she's fine now."

Horror paralyzed Liz. A hundred questions clogged her throat. She finally choked out, "When? What happened?"

"About midnight. Ruth was still up making apple cakes in her *Grossdawdy Haus*. She heard a noise behind her and turned to see a man—a big man with a mask over his head. She screamed and fought him. Her sons-in-law came running and scared him away."

"Thank God." Liz fell back on her pillows, trying not to breathe hard. Dear, spunky Aunt Ruth. Even the thought of someone harming her was obscene. "Did they call the police?"

"No."

"But that doesn't mean I won't," Liz blurted.

"I know." Miriam's calm voice told Liz her cousin actually hoped she would call Chief Houghton.

Miriam told Liz that Phoebe and her husband had insisted Ruth stay with them awhile.

"I still want to check on her." Only throwing her arms around her aunt, touching Ruth's parchment-like cheeks, would ease the whirlpool of fears swirling inside Liz.

"They will be up, doing chores and getting ready for the last day of the festival," Miriam said.

Of course they would. Tears welled in Liz's eyes, yet she couldn't help smiling. Not even an intruder could disrupt their ordered, hardworking lives.

"I know Ruth would welcome your coming."

In the silence that followed, Liz detected an odd hesitation. She pressed, "Are you sure?"

"Oh yes!"

That sounded genuine. Liz's qualms lessened. Yet . . . "Then is there something more I should know?"

Miriam's reluctance spoke volumes. "Amos's horses appeared perfectly fine last night. But one is very ill this morning, possibly dying. Amos thinks the horse may have been poisoned during the night."

Rage overpowered Liz's fears. These crimes could not be random incidents. Her kin had rallied to help her, and someone obviously did not like it. "Thanks for telling me. Please pray that all this stops."

"I will." Miriam uttered Swiss words Liz didn't know, but she understood their blessing.

She called Houghton, who sounded wide awake this early Saturday morning. Did the man ever sleep? She told him about the attacks on Ruth and Amos, ostensibly targeted because they'd promised to help her.

"Thanks for letting me know." He sounded both grateful and frustrated. "Your relatives won't press charges, even if I get enough information from them to find these crooks. But I can't let this kind of thing slide."

Liz considered telling him about Rose. But did she have specific evidence that implicated her? She'd only guessed Trent was the object of Rose's futile affection. As Liz got dressed, she decided to wait a day or two. By then, maybe her relatives' probing might reveal solid evidence.

She beat Houghton to Phoebe's. The minute she crossed the threshold into Phoebe's spotless, bacon-fragrant kitchen, she knew she'd done the right thing. Aunt Ruth, with a glad cry, threw her arms around Liz and clung to her. But her eyes grew fierce when Liz asked her if she and Amos had talked to other workers at the SAG halfway point.

"Yes, during the festival yesterday. No one saw anything." Aunt Ruth crossed her arms. "But apparently, someone thinks otherwise."

A wave of regret swelled in Liz, threatening to overwhelm her. "I'm so, so sorry. I shouldn't have involved you at all."

Aunt Ruth held up a hand. "You have done nothing wrong. It is those who commit *Mord* who should tremble before *Gött*. Now sit. Eat with me."

Liz stayed long enough to polish off bacon and eggs and coax her relatives into talking to the chief. "I want to drop by Uncle Amos's before I fuel those cyclists for the race today."

Her uncle, stoic as ever, said little during Liz's brief stop. But his eyes moistened when he told her the vet's prognosis for his beloved horse was poor. "Still, we must hope for the best."

A tinge of worry crossed his face when he mentioned his sister Ruth. "Take care, Liz. This man may also seek to attack you."

She promised to be careful and made him promise to talk to Chief Houghton.

As Liz drove home, her mind—assured of her relatives' safety for now at least—unfroze. Who was this oversize intruder?

She turned cold all over. Berky?

Surely not. He'd seemed such a teddy bear during that late-night talk on her bench. She still couldn't believe Berky would kill Trent by the granola-bar method. But Rose might. Both shared strong motives to murder the racer. Had Berky somehow formed an alliance with Rose to do Trent in—then attempted to keep Liz's relatives from learning the truth?

She couldn't imagine anything much more bizarre.

Who else would fit Aunt Ruth's description of her assailant?

Reuben Stoltzfus? Liz recalled the man's taller-than-average height, his broad shoulders, and overall big build. Liz blinked at the thought that an Amish man would attack her aunt. Yet, humiliated by Rose's loyalty to a faithless English love, had Reuben considered Ruth and Amos traitors to the community when they questioned Amish race volunteers? Traitors that might reveal Rose as a murderer?

Or had Reuben himself tainted those granola bars?

The sight of the inn's parking lot startled her, as if she hadn't seen it before. Thankfully, her autopilot driving hadn't resulted in an accident. Her pulse still pounded at her horrendous ponderings, but she'd have to calm down and corral her thoughts for now. She had to concentrate on her busy morning—and not look Berky in the eye too many times.

First, she changed Sarah's assignment from cleaning to helping cook and serve. Fluffy scrambled eggs, baked oatmeal with maple syrup, and juicy baked apples with walnuts made a hearty breakfast.

Fortunately, Berky was focused on his food as usual.

"Good luck!" Liz waved to the cyclists as they donned helmets and rode toward the Kappel Apple Race starting line.

They waved back.

How Liz hoped this race would end better for Kandy. For everyone.

With Trent dead and Jason in jail, she couldn't bear to watch the men's time trial. But the Material Girls—minus Mary Ann, who was watching the store—gathered at the start to cheer for Caitlyn, Kandy, Stephanie, and Jessi.

So did the bikers. Even Big Berky, an alien among slim, sleek cyclists, showed up to support the "Olde Mansion Inn Team." Liz watched from the corner of her eye as he pumped his hammy fists and yelled for them. Had Berky really come to show such uncharacteristic camaraderie? Or was this another part of his teddy-bear deception?

Though the men's race results seemed anticlimactic without Trent and Jason, the women's event was as fun and exciting as originally advertised. Kandy, sprinting at the finish as if pursued by her demons, won, with Jessi third. Stephanie and Caitlyn both posted personal bests. In celebration, the cyclists, bikers, and supporters all bought golden, crisp, dinner-plate-sized tenderloin sandwiches, an Indiana specialty.

"Yay, Olde Mansion Team!" Sadie hollered as she slathered hers with mustard and pucker-worthy homemade dill pickles.

"You girls rode enough for all of us, so I don't feel guilty eating this," Liz rationalized.

Any residue of calorie conscience departed with the first bite. How had she lived the past week without one of these?

Their impromptu picnic under the Kappel Apple Tree almost made Liz forget the earlier events of the day. Almost.

Now, as she and Sadie walked back to the inn, she hit a familiar wall. What to do now? Liz cringed at the prospect of wrestling anew with the unruly herd of "maybes" she'd locked away earlier. Especially her doubts about Berky.

A stream of festivalgoers, both townspeople and tourists, flowed through the front door of the inn.

"What in the world?" Liz exclaimed.

"We're trying out an end-of-festival sale. Mary Ann needs help." Sadie zipped inside.

Liz paused to talk to a friend or two, eventually following Sadie inside. She halted in the foyer as more customers marched past to the shop. She shouldn't procrastinate—the pantry was a disaster—but she found herself surrendering to the word *sale* and salivating over the thought of Sew Welcome's lovely wares. She dropped in regularly for coffee and a chat, but she hadn't really seen the newest quilts and other items.

"What do you think I should do, Beans?" She cast a glimpse toward his rug.

No Beans. Had all the commotion actually disturbed his noon nap?

A vague flower bed alert went off in her head, but she ignored it. He'd probably found Bulldog and was enjoying a few extra peanut butter sandwiches before the biker went home tomorrow.

"It's about time you showed up." Mary Ann, reveling in the shop's party atmosphere and its swelling profits, rang up purchases with relish.

Liz scrutinized a rustic, autumn-colored log cabin quilt and a whimsical appliquéd apple-corn-pumpkin wall hanging with basket motifs. The Christmas Corner featured elf pajamas for the entire family, complete with nightcaps, and a breathtaking gold, silver, and red poinsettia quilt. She ran her fingers lightly over its gorgeous folds. Ooh, she could spend the whole afternoon here.

A whine pulled her gaze to the flannel section.

Tail wagging, Beans had cornered, of all people, the Stoltzfus sisters.

"Beans! What are you doing in here?" Liz grabbed his collar. *Five minutes of freedom. Is that too much to ask?*

Beans apparently thought so. He ignored Liz and almost knocked Rose down, nosing her knees. He even jumped up on her, frantically licking her shawl.

Mattie pushed at Beans in vain. "Shoo! Go away!"

Meanwhile, Rose stood like an Amish mannequin, pink mouth frozen in a terrified *O*.

"Here, boy!" Sadie unscrewed his "treat" peanut butter jar she now kept in Sew Welcome.

At the sound, the bulldog turned, tail wagging even more furiously. Sadie dipped a big spoonful. "Come on, Beans!"

He gave Rose one more sniff, then bounded toward Sadie like a puppy. She led him through a gauntlet of mostly laughing customers back to his rug.

Liz apologized to Rose. "Are you hurt?"

"I did not know you allowed the dog in the shop." Mattie glowered. "Rose is afraid of dogs."

Is this the same young woman? "He usually isn't in here. I'm so sorry," Liz babbled.

Rose still hadn't moved. Liz reached toward her, then stopped. What could she do to bring the young woman back to life?

"I am not hurt." Rose finally spoke. "But I want to go home."

Mattie said to Liz, her tone still icy, "Do you have a different door outside? We don't want to walk past that dog again."

"Certainly." Liz guided them out the back door, still apologizing.

When she returned to check on Beans, he was sprawled on his back in his usual spot, looking more relaxed than he had a right to be. Since Sadie wasn't around, Liz scolded him. "Bad dog!"

She didn't expect Beans to stir, and he didn't.

What had gotten into him? Beans wasn't an aggressive dog, except with Bulldog, his special buddy. And with Liz when he begged for her peanut butter sandwich.

Peanut butter.

Of course. Beans had smelled peanut butter on Rose.

Or peanut something.

Sew Welcome customers waved to Liz as they exited.

She smiled automatically, her mind churning. She attempted to calm it. Rose could have eaten PB&J for lunch. Perhaps Beans had smelled a few crumbs clinging to her clothes. Or maybe she'd made peanut butter cookies for the festival.

Liz tried not to let her imagination run away with her, but her mind refused to rest. Rose also could have spilled peanut oil on the shawl. Perhaps while doctoring Trent's bag at the halfway point?

She attempted to shake the possibility from her thoughts. But one realization etched itself on the wall of her mind as if burned there: Whatever Rose had spilled, however she'd spilled it, Rose would wash the shawl soon. Maybe today.

Especially if she now realized its peanut oil stain could point toward her guilt. She'd scrub away that evidence with strong lye soap and throw it out with the wash water.

All right, all right. I'll call Houghton. Anything to quiet the relentless whispers in her head, whispers growing into shouts. It wasn't like she hadn't told him her weird hunches before.

An accusation against Rose, even a very tentative one, would prove enough excitement for today. She wouldn't mention Berky or Reuben as suspects who might have attacked Ruth.

Slipping inside her quarters, Liz called Houghton.

He listened willingly, but as she related the Beans incident, he spattered her account with disinterested comments: "Beans? Oh, your dog. Peanut butter? Really?" Then, *Rose Stoltzfus?*"

At his last reply, she held her phone away from her ear. She stuttered, "I-I know it seems impossible."

"That the little Amish mouse murdered somebody? *Yeah.*"

Liz countered, "Stranger things have happened."

He harrumphed. "Maybe on the science fiction channel."

This wasn't going well. Liz cajoled and pleaded, stopping short of bribery. "Just talk to Rose for a few minutes."

Finally, the chief agreed. "I'm not sure what I'll say. The Amish don't like courtesy calls from the police. Her dad isn't exactly my favorite bowling buddy."

Talk to Rose about Reuben's abuse, Liz wanted to say. Yet, repugnant as Rose's father's actions were, murder was worse. "They're aware of what's been going on. They know you've questioned many SAG volunteers. Ask Rose a few questions as you would any other," she urged. "Mattie, too, if you don't want to seem as if you're persecuting her sister. If your instincts don't sense something, I'll shut up."

Static rattled in Liz's phone as Houghton exhaled. "All right. But about shutting up? Practice that. Now." He hung up.

Trying not to feel insulted, Liz hung up too. After working together on several cases, maybe the chief was treating her like family. Like an annoying little sister. A kid sister with a big, big imagination.

Gritting her teeth, she decided to clean the pantry, as she was in a bad mood anyway.

She'd emptied canned goods and staples from two walls of shelves when her cell phone rang.

Houghton.

Did she really want to hear his dad voice telling her to drop it? Sighing, Liz sat on a stool, pushed back her messy hair, and answered it. "You were right."

She nearly fell backward. "What?"

"I've taken Rose Stoltzfus into custody. She confessed to killing Trent Cleveland."

18

"**O**ne of those Amish girls killed Trent?" Jessi's eyes widened until they looked like big green marbles.

A murmur of disbelief spread among cyclists and bikers alike. For the moment, even the sweet rolls Naomi had contributed to coffee hour were forgotten.

"I'm afraid so." Liz still found it hard to believe. Though she didn't know Rose well, the young woman's confession continued to rumble inside her like an aftershock. Liz described the strange events at Sew Welcome and her phone call from Chief Houghton informing her of Rose's arrest.

"We knew Trent had Amish girlfriends," Stephanie said, "but I never imagined one of them would murder him."

Kandy, sitting next to Liz, said nothing.

Liz squeezed her hand. "It's over," she said softly.

Kandy took a deep breath, then nodded slowly as she exhaled. "After racing this morning, I don't feel like riding. But I'd like to take a walk alone down by the lake."

"Good idea." What a tangle of emotions the young woman must be feeling. Liz hugged Kandy and breathed a prayer for her as she left.

Gradually the conversation lightened, and the gathering morphed from somber to celebratory. The mystery was solved and their friends freed from suspicion.

"Good old Beans." Bulldog fed the adoring canine another sandwich. "You are awesome, boy! The best detective in town."

Liz let that one slide.

"Yay, Beans!" The group cheered and laughed and took pictures with the hero of the hour.

The spotlight centered on Beans, and Liz didn't mind at all. Like Kandy, she breathed a huge sigh of relief.

She reminded herself to be grateful that Aunt Ruth had not been injured in her home invasion. Even Uncle Amos's horse had defied all predictions and was getting better by the hour. Still, for Liz, the tension would not end until the arrest of her relatives' assailant.

And Berky hadn't shown up. Unease rippled through her as coffee hour neared its end.

"Maybe he's already headed to Wildton for the night," Shine suggested. "A little earlier than usual, but he really likes a bar over there, the Texas Tenderloin and Tattoo. He calls it the Triple T."

"Yeah, since he and Honey broke up, Berky's been going there a lot," Bulldog said. "Usually stays half the night."

Including the night of Aunt Ruth's attack? Liz's pulse accelerated. As far as she knew, Houghton hadn't yet questioned the biker. *Unless he's grilling him right now.* She bit her lip. But if the chief had any evidence against Berky, Liz believed Houghton would have told her. The chief probably couldn't stop him from leaving town tomorrow.

If Liz could nail down a firm alibi, the biker could ride home with nothing hanging over his head. And she would know he really was the giant teddy bear who would never hurt an old lady.

A phone call to Houghton, and maybe he would fill in the blanks for Liz.

Maybe.

Some restlessness inside her demanded she know for herself.

Liz walked to Sew Welcome and found Sadie cleaning up. "What are you doing tonight?"

Liz hadn't listed riding Pink Penelope—or any motorcycle—on her bucket list, but then, she hadn't listed a visit to the Texas Tenderloin and Tattoo either. Other than for alliteration's sake, why would someone name an Indiana bar "Texas"? Liz pondered this for some minutes, glad to keep her mind off the way Sadie floored the motorcycle.

She'd never admit it to her friend, but there was something exhilarating about flying past trees, houses, and cows as if they were scenic background, painted for their benefit. She'd underestimated, though, how the chilly October wind nearly paralyzed her. Liz clung to Sadie for warmth more than out of fear of their increasing speed.

At least that was what she told herself.

Was Sadie hitting potholes for the thrill? When Penelope had the back roads to herself, Sadie didn't bother staying in her lane.

Of course, she'd never endanger their lives. Liz knew that.

Still, she gave silent thanks when Sadie veered into the Triple T's parking lot. Liz smothered a scream as Sadie roared to a gravel-spitting stop, almost in the bar's doorway.

Liz forced her rubbery knees to dismount, wondering why she hadn't called Houghton instead.

"Great ride, right?" Sadie threw open the heavy wooden door, and the sad twang of a breakup song drifted out. "Come on, girl. Let's do this."

Liz's first glimpse inside the bar didn't help matters. The growing twilight outside seemed bright compared to the smoky darkness within, lit only by TV screens and squiggly orange, yellow, and green neon signs. People were lumps and clumps, scattered throughout the room.

None of the lumps appeared big enough to be Berky.

Liz had taken photos at the race this morning, photos that included the biker. Would showing them around do any good? Despite his size and frequent visits, could anyone have actually *seen* his face?

Now a divorce song played in the background so loud that Liz's teeth vibrated. Not exactly a cheery atmosphere. But it was the perfect place for a guy in a pity-party mood.

Sadie, far more sure-footed than Liz, tugged her toward the bar and ordered two diet colas and a basket of fried pickles for them to share.

Liz had never tasted them before, and she didn't want to now. Especially now. "Seriously, Sadie, fried pickles after all that fair food?" Her friend shrugged.

Liz turned her attention to the bartender, who plopped down their drinks. The TV aura outlined his silhouette. She wished she could see his eyes, but only neon lights reflected off his glasses. She held out the picture of Berky on her phone. "Excuse me. I wonder if you could help us—"

"I'll help you, pretty lady." A sinewy arm slid around her waist. "Any way you want."

"No thanks." Liz shot the tall, thin guy her best withering glare and edged away.

Or tried to. The arm, like a boa constrictor, curled around her even tighter. She elbowed the man. "I said, *no*—"

"Leave my friend alone." Sadie's usually smiley tone sounded deadly.

A nasty, beer-laced laugh. "You must be her ma. You gonna stop me, old lady?"

"Yeah."

Liz didn't know exactly what happened, but she heard a sickening *crunch*, a thud, and a cry of pain. Bent over, the guy clutched his foot, swearing. She guessed his anguish had something to do with Sadie's high-heeled, pointy-toed cowboy boots. Bringing Sadie had been a good move.

The man limped away.

"Now," Sadie said to the bartender, "you want to help my friend?"

"Okay." A bland, disinterested tone.

Liz held out her phone. "Have you seen this man?"

"Sure. Seen him almost every day this week."

Cautious joy surged through her. "Did you see him late last night?"

He snorted. "It was all-you-can-eat tenderloin night. That dude snarfed down eight sandwiches. A new record."

Liz smothered a laugh. "Do you remember how late he stayed?"

A pause. "Well, we ran out of tenderloins about two in the morning. He wanted another one. When I told him we was out, he left. Probably two thirty or so."

"Thank you." *Thank you! Thank you!* Liz wanted to dance. But if another patron misjudged her intentions, Sadie's boots might get busy again.

The fried pickles turned out to be surprisingly tasty. Liz was munching her second one when Sadie cut loose and joined line dancers, stepping into the smoky gloom as if they possessed radar.

Though Liz hadn't done much line dancing, it was too dark for anyone to notice her miscues. She moved into a line, and she and Sadie clapped, turned, and stomped their way through three more rhythmic breakup songs.

No one bothered them.

If Sadie was an exuberant biker on the way here, she pulled out the stops—and ran through several others—on the ride home. Liz, under the influence of fried pickles, threw out a few "yee-haws!" as well, loving the echo as they roared through underpasses.

As they buzzed past the Pleasant Creek town limits sign, they quieted, and Sadie slowed Penelope to within ten miles per hour of the speed limit. Liz's body reminded her that she'd been up since before dawn. Her weariness guaranteed that she'd sleep well tonight, better than other nights this week.

Then Sadie pulled into the parking lot, and Liz caught sight of a large shadow fleeing through her backyard.

19

With Berky's one-armed hug, Liz's toes left the ground.

"That was the best breakfast I've ever eaten. Thanks for everything." Standing beside his bike near the inn's front entrance, he mumbled, "Not sure I coulda made it through last week without all you did."

"Come again," she gasped, stretching to reach the sidewalk. The guy might sport a potbelly, but he also had muscles. His arm had nearly squeezed her in two. Thankfully, he soon set her down.

"We'll be back next year for the Hog Wild Ride." Berky huffed like a giant bellows. "Who knows? Maybe Honey will get a brain by then."

Liz doubted that, but she said, "You know you'll be welcome."

"Man, it's good to be out from under all the hassle. Free to go home when I want to."

He didn't know she'd cleared him completely with Houghton last night, but that was okay.

None of her guests knew about Houghton's finding big footprints under the inn's windows, but since they were leaving, she'd decided not to mention it. Reuben now topped her suspect list, and after everybody left, she hoped to discuss that at length with the chief.

Berky opened his arms and smiled, basking in the morning sunshine. As he dropped his arms to his sides, the biker's smile disappeared. "Rough gig for that poor Amish girl, though. Cleveland messed her around like he did every other lady within riding distance."

His eyes sparked, so Liz hastened to change the subject. When would their club ride again?

They were chatting away when Shine and Pixie joined them. As they exchanged good-byes, Liz realized she would miss them too.

Inwardly, she chuckled. Who would have thought that she could click with biker babes? Or line dance at the Triple T, for that matter?

"Wait for us!" Sadie yelled from the front door. "Beans and I want to ride with you guys to Marion!" She and the bulldog had dressed for the occasion, resplendent in their magenta-and-silver outfits. As usual, Beans was glued to Bulldog, who pulled a last peanut butter sandwich from his pocket.

"I'm going to miss you, boy." The biker dropped it into Beans's wide-open mouth.

The dog gulped the treat with a shiver of delight that started at his big, pushed-in face and wiggled to the end of his stubby tail.

"He'll miss you too." Sadie grinned. "He won't sweet-talk nearly as much peanut butter out of me."

Ha. Liz knew Beans could coax Sadie out of her life savings if he wanted to.

The bikers headed toward the parking lot. Liz waved, wincing as the sun lit the studs and sequins on Sadie's and Beans's costumes. The motorcycles awoke, roaring. The group zoomed past with Beans wearing a pink helmet and Doggles, riding in Sadie's sidecar as she propelled Pink Penelope down Main Street. Thinking of her ride with Sadie last night, Liz understood why he might tolerate the indignity of his outfit.

Much of downtown had returned to its usual sleepy Sunday appearance. How could a festival that drew thousands of attendees shrink overnight, as if banished by a genie? The square appeared empty, but she welcomed the clock tower's music, which carnival noises had drowned out for a week.

Already, the inn seemed a little empty too. Liz poured herself a cup of coffee, planning her Sunday. She'd clean up the brunch mess, of course, but leave most of the heavy housework for tomorrow. In case a traveler passed through Pleasant Creek later today, she'd tidy one guest room and change the linens.

Some other room besides the Somewhere in Time Room, where Trent and Jason had stayed.

She gulped. Jason, expecting to ride in yesterday's race, had paid for the room through today. His belongings were still there. Cleared of murder charges by Rose's confession, he would post bail this morning. She hoped he'd come by and pick up his stuff, but she didn't want to face that prospect either.

Liz sighed. Remembering the chief's grim face last night, would she be able to quiet her mind and heart this afternoon? Take the nap she craved? Surely, last night's unwelcome visitor would not attempt anything during broad daylight. She promised herself to avoid the subject for the next few hours. And since she'd missed church this morning—an occupational hazard when the inn was full of guests—she'd go to a home Bible study tonight.

Liz glanced out a window and saw the cyclists loading bikes and bags into their van. They appeared to be walking toward the front entrance. Good! Not all guests wanted a personal good-bye, but having survived this tough week together, Liz had wanted to touch base with the women.

Kandy strode up the front sidewalk. "I'll never forget what a friend you've been through this whole ordeal." The Kappel Apple Race women's champion gave Liz a good-bye hug. Clear-eyed, with head high, she hardly resembled the beaten-down young woman who had first arrived at the Olde Mansion Inn. Liz hoped Kandy would never have another toxic relationship again.

Jessi and Stephanie chimed in their thanks. Jessi said, "If you hadn't found out about Trent and that Amish girl, the police might never have realized Kandy was innocent."

Liz waved off their lavish kudos. "Houghton's an excellent police chief. I just happened to stumble on a few oddities that wouldn't go away. And Rose, like Jason, isn't a very good liar." Liz told them about Jason's posting bail.

"Maybe we should go down to the jail to meet him," Kandy said.

"Why? I'm not sure I want to see him again." Stephanie's dark eyes glinted. "I hate dopers."

"I do too." Kandy grimaced. "But even if Jason escapes a jail sentence, he'll be banned from racing for a long time. Maybe permanently." She looked from Jessi to Stephanie to Liz. "Jason needs friends now more than ever."

The other two exchanged reluctant glances.

Jessi rolled her eyes. But she said, "Okay. If it works out to see him, I'll try."

"Me too." Stephanie paused. "But he rode here in Trent's van, didn't he? I don't want him to ride home with us."

"We don't have room for him and his bike anyway," Kandy admitted, "but I still think it's important we let him know he's not alone."

"I'll call and see when he's being released." Liz talked to Officer Dixon, Houghton's right-hand man. She also found out the chief would be in around four. Liz told the women, "His paperwork's gone through. Jason should be freed within the next half hour."

She offered them leftover sweet rolls, not wanting to be left alone with several of Naomi's delectable creations.

They groaned in unison.

Stephanie said, "After your amazing brunch, I don't need a thing."

"True, but maybe we can split a couple." Jessi cast a longing look toward the inn. "And I could use more coffee for the road."

As they ate their snacks, Liz said, "Do you mind if I go with you to see Jason?"

Kandy looked relieved. "Maybe you can help us think of what to say."

Not sure of that. Walking with them downtown, Liz searched for some positive comment to bestow on Jason. "At least you didn't kill Trent"?

She preferred to ponder Rose's confession. If Liz could connect with the chief later, maybe he would tell her more. He'd told her very little last night, focusing on her prowler.

They sat in the austere waiting area while Officer Dixon brought out Jason. Gray-faced, he stared at the women as if he couldn't believe his eyes. They stared back.

Liz let out a weak, "Hi." *Brilliant. Yeah, I know exactly what to say.*

"Hi." Jason's sounded weaker.

She fumbled, "Want to come pick up your stuff?"

"Uh, yeah, I guess." Now he was looking everywhere but at them.

Kandy stood. "How are you?"

Jason shrugged and gazed at the floor. "I'm okay. Glad to get out. At least for a while."

The walls seemed to close in on Liz. They all needed to breathe. Liz took his arm as she would have Steve's. "Let's go outside."

Amazing, the restorative power of a few rays of sunshine and clear autumn air. Little was said, but heads lifted. Liz steered the group toward the clock tower, surrounded by brilliant patchwork beds of chrysanthemums.

Jason opened his arms as Berky had. "Whoa. Better than vitamins."

The women cyclists gaped at him.

"*Some* vitamins, maybe." Jessi's feline eyes sparked.

He clapped his hands to his head. "I'm sorry. Stupid, stupid! I said . . . I did a really *stupid* thing."

"You're right about that." Stephanie's sweet face hardened. "I never figured you for a doper."

His shoulders wilted. His voice shriveled. "I never thought I'd be one either."

So far, this reconciliation wasn't going very well. Liz lowered her chin to catch Jason's eye. "You're not the first person to make bad choices. But with the help of God and friends, you can somehow make the best of this."

Kandy locked her gaze on him from the other side. "Maybe we could help you. Depending on how things work out."

Jason didn't look at her, but he nodded.

Kandy glanced at the other two cyclists.

"Okay." Stephanie's red-faced anger had quieted.

"We'll see." At least Jessi didn't look like she wanted to run over him now.

Liz squeezed his arm. "Why don't you come with us back to the inn? There are a couple of Naomi's sweet rolls with your name on them."

"For real?" For the first time, Jason resembled the fresh-faced young man who had come to Pleasant Creek for the Kappel Apple Race.

Once there, the women cyclists said quick good-byes and left.

Jason sat in the breakfast nook and devoured sweet rolls while Liz finished straightening the kitchen. "Man, I haven't tasted anything near this good since before—"

"Enjoy." She knew he couldn't bear to say the word *jail*.

"Look, I'll do my best to find a rental car today and get out of your hair. But the nearest place is probably Marion, right? Do you think you could give me a ride there?"

"Probably." Liz glanced at the back door. Caitlyn had just arrived. "But first, I think you need to talk to someone."

20

Caitlyn wasn't going to be nicey-nice about this, Liz saw. Her friend had set her jaw and wore an expression the most stubborn patient might fear. When Jason saw Caitlyn, his hangdog look returned with a vengeance.

Liz excused herself. Rather than shiver out on her bench—clouds had dulled the azure sky—she headed for her quarters and a nice, long nap. When she awoke, she found them gone and a note from Caitlyn. Jason had rented a van in Marion, and Caitlyn had borrowed the Sew Welcome van to take him and his bike there. The thought of Jason riding in that gaudy, girlie vehicle with Caitlyn, the compassionate dragon, almost gave her a smile.

He'd written his own boyish note of thanks that made her think of Steve. Eyes moist, she prayed, *Oh, Lord, please help him weather this.*

If Jason wound up in court, she intended to be there.

Right now, though, she wanted to talk to Chief Houghton about Rose. Maybe he'd permit her to visit the young woman, who probably didn't know which way to turn. Most Amish rejected legal representation. But would Rose's desperation open her to a lawyer's help?

Not that Liz wanted to practice law again—especially since she possessed only corporate, not criminal, experience. Rose's father certainly wouldn't pay for a private attorney. Perhaps Liz could coax Rose into asking for a public defender.

Liz scowled as she walked through the slumbering downtown. Reuben may not have tampered with Trent's granola bars, but with Rose's arrest, she suspected his influence more than ever.

Would Rose have committed murder alone? No way. She also fit the profile of the ideal scapegoat: naive, probably guilt-ridden, and unaccustomed to defending herself, especially to her father. The whole scenario presented an even more sinister variation on Reuben's theme of abuse.

Last night's episode had only confirmed in her mind that Reuben wasn't done yet. The sooner they caught him, the better.

She stifled a shiver as she entered the police station. Such a plain, forbidding building amid the other charming ones, with their Swiss chalet decor. She'd spent more time here than she ever had at Boston PDs.

The chief raised an eyebrow as she entered. "Thought for once you'd take a day off. Haven't you had enough excitement for one festival?"

"That's funny. I thought you might too." Liz pasted a small grin on her face. "Be assured, I don't plan to lift a finger this evening."

"Me either. Once I get through this paperwork." He shoved piles of forms and folders aside. "Dixon will patrol your inn tonight. He's downright ticked that big guy got past us. I am too."

"He got lucky." They couldn't guard her every minute. But knowing she'd be alone in the inn tonight, Liz shivered again. "I might ask Naomi to stay with me."

"Good idea." Houghton seemed to know she wanted to change the subject. "Suppose you want to hear all the dirt on Rose Stoltzfus. Though I imagine you know almost as much as I do."

"Yes, please."

"She'd thought this through real well. More than once, she'd packed picnic baskets for her and Cleveland to eat out in the woods. Knew all about his peanut allergy. Volunteered at the halfway point to help fix food. She fixed his all right." He harrumphed. "Skimmed oil from her homemade peanut butter because she thought he wouldn't detect the peanut taste as easily. Sneaked Cleveland's bag off to the side and doctored his granola bars using a skinny straw."

Had Rose planned these careful details? Or Reuben? Liz was inclined to believe the latter, even if Rose had carried them out.

The chief continued, "Rose told me that until this year, she'd really believed Cleveland would eventually join the Amish and marry her."

Liz thought of Kandy's initial blindness, of her own self-delusion when she was dating Matt. "Rose wanted to believe he loved her."

"Picked a loser, for sure. Not surprising, with the dad she has." Houghton's eyes sparked. "I'm wondering if Reuben might have been involved, at least in trying to silence your relatives. The big perp your aunt described certainly could have been him. He might have been your prowler too."

So she and the chief were on the same page.

"I hope and pray some tiny part of him actually wanted to protect his daughter and keep her out of jail." Houghton cleared his throat. Twice. Despite years of police work, he was a family man, a doting grandpa, she'd heard. He still struggled with the pain of those he pursued.

The chief quickly reverted to his official tone. "More likely, Reuben was trying to preserve what family pride he had left. A daughter with an English boyfriend was bad enough. A daughter jailed for murder would be the worst—especially if she charged Reuben with abuse to gain a jury's sympathy." His voice sharpened. "He says he was in bed the night your relatives were attacked—hard to confirm or refute. He was home last night too. Mattie confirmed that, but who knows what threats he's made to his daughters?"

"He hasn't visited Rose, has he?" Liz asked, but she already knew the answer.

Houghton shook his head.

Incarceration meant immediate shunning by the Amish community, including close relatives, but Reuben probably would have distanced himself from his daughter to protect his own skin.

Suddenly tired, Liz propped her face on her hand. "Has anyone visited Rose?"

"Her sister sneaked by for a few minutes. Miriam too, but she said Rose clammed up." He shrugged. "Now Rose doesn't want to see anyone."

"Then she probably won't see me."

"No." His keen gaze morphed into a kind one. "Why don't you forget all this for the rest of the evening and enjoy your Sunday? You've had a rough way to go."

That sounded so good . . . "Maybe I'll do that."

"Be sure you do." Houghton gave her a fatherly pat on the shoulder.

As she wandered home, Liz realized she hadn't eaten anything since breakfast. She zapped leftover chicken rice soup in the microwave and, before she realized it, devoured half a box of crackers topped with squares of baby Swiss cheese. *Oink!*

"I hope they don't have refreshments tonight," she mumbled as she pulled up to the home where the Bible study would be held.

Futile optimism. If she didn't know better, she'd think membership at Pleasant Creek Community Church included mandatory participation in the Pillsbury Bake-Off.

Sure enough, the hostess had baked chocolate eclairs. A polite guest had to eat at least one, didn't she? At first, the talk over refreshments circled again and again around Rose Stoltzfus's confession, winding up Liz like a child's toy. The leader, however, steered everyone toward prayer for all involved. Eventually, the Scriptures they studied, plus the warmth of the group, nurtured Liz's weary heart and mind.

Naomi was going to Indianapolis to visit family tonight, so Liz picked up the key to Sweet Everything. She didn't know how she would deal with her shivers tomorrow, but tonight she intended to get a solid night's sleep. She flopped on the comfy twin bed in Naomi's back room and zonked out like a tired ten-year-old.

The next morning, Miriam's call interrupted Liz just after she'd returned to her inn and had begun a leisurely cleanup.

Hearing from Miriam couldn't be good. As much as she loved her cousin, Liz didn't want to hear anything negative. She made herself answer.

"Would you come see me today?" Miriam's usually serene voice held a note of deep worry. "I need to talk to you about Rose."

The name bounced off Liz. "You visited her, right? What happened?"

Childish voices murmured in the background. Miriam whispered, "I can't talk now."

Liz said, "I'll try to make it by ten or so."

Sarah was off today. Liz yanked sheets from beds, stuffed the big commercial washer, and cleaned two bathrooms. She gulped a mug of her strongest coffee, then took more of the same to Sew Welcome as Mary Ann and Sadie, both dragging, opened the shop.

"No Pink Penelope? No cowboy boots?" Liz tried to lighten her own mood.

"Today I need a rocking chair." Sadie faked a collapse.

"I know the feeling." Liz told them about Miriam's call.

"Whatever can be the matter?" Mary Ann stared. "I thought this whole Trent Cleveland thing was solved."

She'd have to tell them about the prowler. Later. "Miriam's worried. That will worry *me* until I find out what's bothering her."

When she arrived at her cousin's farmhouse, Miriam was waiting in a rocker on the front porch. On a Monday morning—laundry day—that was just downright unnatural.

Liz sat in the rocker across from her. "What's going on?"

"I'm sorry to interrupt your day, but I had to tell someone." Miriam's indigo eyes had clouded to gray. "I went to see Rose Stoltzfus last night."

"How did you manage that?" Liz knew how Miriam's husband would feel about a jail visitation.

"Philip and the boys left last evening to travel north of Fort Wayne for a barn raising today. I asked Sarah to stay with the children while I went to the police station." Tears welled in Miriam's eyes. "Rose's mother and I were friends when her daughters were small. Rose was such a sweet little girl. I-I could not bear the thought of her sitting in that jail alone."

Liz clasped her cousin's hand and told her about her discussion with Houghton. "Did Rose say something the chief didn't hear?"

"No, it wasn't what she said." Miriam picked at her apron pocket with her other hand. "It was how she looked."

"How she looked?" Liz searched Miriam's downcast face. Had Rose's father slapped her around before her arrest? Or had another prisoner victimized her?

"No, no, physically, she was fine." Miriam had read Liz's mind. "It was her expression."

She'd expected something a bit more substantial from her levelheaded cousin. Something that would warrant a rare phone call.

Pain raked Miriam's face. "Rose wore the same kind of expression Isaac did when he confessed to murder. He lied to protect us and Sarah." She raised her chin. "Rose is protecting someone. I am sure of it. She did *not* murder that cyclist."

Liz hardly knew what to say. Had that traumatic episode hurt Miriam so much that she was reading her son's past suffering into Rose's face? Houghton would see it that way. Or maybe Miriam was being swayed by her relationship with Rose's mother.

But her cousin did nothing without weighing her thoughts and actions carefully.

Liz patted her shoulder. "You've thought this through, haven't you?"

Miriam nodded, dabbing her eyes. "I could not sleep last night. I tried to dismiss my impression. I prayed I would see only the truth." Her shoulders straightened. "I believe I have."

Doubt pulled on Liz. Miriam's insistence of Rose's innocence was strictly intuitive. Yet what her cousin said about Rose protecting someone might make sense . . . Was she protecting her father?

A pool of magma boiled inside Liz. Why would Rose try to keep *him* out of jail?

Fear? Maybe he'd threatened her. Or perhaps, like many abuse victims, Rose simply could not free herself from Reuben's controlling influence.

When Liz admitted she'd suspected Reuben of killing Trent and that she and Houghton considered him a suspect in her aunt's assault, Miriam slowly shook her head. "I do not know Reuben's whereabouts when your aunt was attacked. But I recall that the day before the festival, he was going with several other men to Shipshewana for a few days to buy horses. He asked Philip if he wanted to go. If Reuben went, he was out of town when the young man died."

"Do you remember the other men's names?" Liz *had* to check out that alibi.

Miriam scrunched her face. "Not at the moment. Perhaps they will come to me. I really do not want to ask Philip."

No, Philip would want to know why. Liz sighed. Today was nothing like the relaxed Monday she'd hoped to savor.

At that moment, Keturah danced out the front door and hugged Liz.

Miriam chided her young daughter gently, then invited Liz in for cider. "I am sorry to have kept you on this chilly porch with nothing hot to drink."

Keturah's older sister Grace had begun to heat spiced cider on the enormous cookstove even before they entered.

Keturah, blessedly oblivious to her elders' tensions, chattered excitedly about the festival and helping at the halfway SAG stop. "I put orange slices on paper plates, and I helped Rose and Mattie with bags of food."

I'm sure you did. Liz grinned.

"There were *bunches* of bags." Keturah frowned. "It was fun until they started arguing about a stupid old shawl. Miss Rose got mad at Miss Mattie for wearing hers without asking. Miss Mattie said mean things. I thought grown-ups didn't act like that."

Mattie wore Rose's shawl at the SAG stop? Liz's breath seemed to coagulate.

Miriam stood stock-still.

"Keturah," Grace reproved in her most adult voice, "you should not spread such gossip."

Instead of reprimanding both, Miriam said, "Grace, did you hear them discuss the shawl?"

"Yes. It is just as Keturah said." When the Stoltzfuses continued to glower at each other, Grace had taken her sister to play with their cousins.

Both girls stared when their mother handed them the unusual late-morning treat of sugar cookies and sent them to the barn to play.

Meanwhile, Liz had managed to suck in enough air so she could speak. "If Rose wore that same shawl to Sew Welcome, Beans detected peanut residue of some sort on it."

"Which means Mattie tampered with the cyclist's food." Miriam's mouth, like her mind, seemed slow to grasp the possibility.

"Or it may mean she ate a peanut butter sandwich sometime that morning. Maybe she's a messy eater like me." Liz silently commanded her pulse to slow. "The shawl has gone to a lab for testing. Even if they find peanut products on it, the shawl was an iffy clue from the start, hardly something that would have resulted in Rose's arrest. Yet she confessed."

"Very quickly," Miriam mused. "Yes, I can see her covering for her sister's actions. Because of their father's harshness, Rose has played that role all her life. Rose used to try to direct her father's anger toward herself rather than her mother." For a second, white-hot anger flared in Miriam's face. She said quietly, "Mattie always was quite impulsive."

"But why would Mattie harm Trent? Do you think he dated both sisters?"

Miriam flinched. "I do not know. From what I have heard about him, it is possible."

Liz exhaled through gritted teeth. *Get over it.* Fury at Trent now seemed stupid, but Liz still couldn't let it go. If the man had used only one brain cell, she and Miriam wouldn't be discussing his murder by Amish sisters who probably had never even read a fictional whodunit.

Miriam tilted her head as she always did when thinking hard. "I doubt if both sisters dated the cyclist. The past three or four years, Rose occasionally has spoken of her English beau. Mattie has not. I have noticed no recent rift between them, other than the usual sister tiffs."

A big question overshadowed any other. Liz said, "Do you think Mattie's loyalty to Rose is so strong she would kill Trent in revenge for how he treated her sister?"

"I do not know if her devotion to family matches Rose's. But Mattie's anger at him could have burst out of control. As I said, she has always been the impulsive one."

How easily a young life could be destroyed. Liz still ached inside at the thought of Jason's downfall. Now it was happening to Rose and maybe Mattie?

"At the least, I believe Rose is hiding something," Miriam declared as if to a jury.

Liz almost grinned. If they'd been legal partners, the two of them working together might have made a killing.

Terrible pun. Any hint of a smile faded as Liz thought of involving Miriam in this appalling case. Even worse, her girls. Were they in danger, even now? Liz's stomach lurched at the idea. "You know that I must tell Chief Houghton about this."

Miriam nodded. "The Bible tells us Gött is just. If Mattie is guilty, Rose should not suffer for her sister's sins."

Liz's relief fought with her fear. "Whoever attacked Aunt Ruth is still out there. Keturah or Grace may have mentioned that shawl conversation to others, and you know how quickly stories like that spread, even in the Amish community. I can't imagine Mattie would harm your girls. But Reuben might. If he's involved and he thinks your girls might know something, I fear for their safety. Especially with Philip gone."

Her cousin's face paled, but she spoke steadily. "We will visit my sister and her husband in Ohio. I will ask my brothers to do the chores until Philip and the boys come home."

"Good!" Liz abandoned the usual side embrace for an all-out hug. "I will pray for you. Be careful."

Miriam returned the hug. "You worry about us and everyone else. But surely the wrongdoers know of your skill in discovering the truth." She drew back, riveting Liz with her troubled gaze. "May Gött protect you as well."

21

If the weather had matched the gorgeous Indian summer days they'd enjoyed during the festival, Liz might have played hooky as she drove home from Miriam's. Perhaps she would have parked her car near the covered bridge that she had biked over with Jackson and breathed in the serene beauty as she pondered the newly hatched craziness of this case.

But nearly torrential rains had swept the area last night, and today, the sky wore a leaden cloak. Thankfully, the gravel road Liz always took back to town hadn't been affected by high water.

Liz frowned as she contemplated the chores that awaited. She expected no guests until Friday, but she'd easily spend the entire week catching up, as would Naomi. Maybe they could take a break together on Thursday . . .

What was that? A quarter of a mile ahead, a buggy had pulled over. But it was parked at an odd angle. Was it stuck in a ditch?

Liz stopped a short distance behind the buggy. Jumping out, she hurried toward it, noting the back wheels were sunk halfway in mud. A team of huge farm horses shifted and whickered nervously in front. A small young woman in Amish dress held the horses and waved frantically to Liz.

Mattie Stoltzfus.

Liz's heart leaped like a frightened deer. Her stomach plummeted.

"Thanks be to Gött that you came this way!" Mattie's scared face, now awash with relief, rebuked Liz's fears.

"Uh, yeah." Slowly, Liz pulled out her cell phone.

"Please do not call anyone." Mattie's anxiety rose several notches. "They will tell *Vater*."

A typical teenage response to a driving mishap. But in Mattie's case, a valid desire for secrecy. Pocketing her phone, Liz said, "What happened?"

"Motorcycles spooked my horses. They swerved the buggy off the road. I managed to get this far out of the ditch, but I can't free the back wheels."

"That doesn't sound like it was your fault."

Mattie's shoulders slumped. She didn't answer.

Never had a person looked less capable of murder. Instead of doctoring Trent's granola bars, maybe Mattie *had* merely eaten a peanut butter sandwich at the SAG stop.

Liz wanted to turn and run, but she asked, "Is there something I can do to help?"

Mattie clasped her hands. "Could you guide the horses forward? If I push the back of the buggy, I think that will free the wheels."

The plan might work if a strong man pushed with all his might. But Mattie alone? Nope. Liz doubted the two of them could budge this buggy from that black, sucking mud. Plus, the horses still seemed jittery, as if expecting more motorcycles to roar by.

Liz screwed up her courage and clutched the harnesses where Mattie indicated, close to their noses. At least she hadn't yet included Liz in the muddy, gunky part of her scheme. When their efforts failed, surely Mattie would be more open to calling for help.

Liz had grown accustomed to the constant presence of horses in her town and on her relatives' farms. But she'd never stood this close to them before. Muscles rippled under smooth brown coats as the horses stamped and snorted. Big, wild eyes stared at her accusingly.

A long, snakelike lash whistled through the air, slashing one horse's back. With a shriek, he rose on powerful hind legs, yanking Liz into the air. She lost her grip and hit gravel. "Stop, Mattie! You're scaring—"

Crack! Huge, muscled chests above her plunged up and down. The ground shook as anvil hooves rained down around Liz. She tried to crawl away.

Crack!

Mattie stood to the side. Smiling?

Agony exploded in Liz's head, and she knew no more.

———— *//////////////////////////////////* ————

A door creaked, and a sliver of bright light hurt Liz's eyes. She was lying on her back, head and chest propped up. Who could sleep like this? Her annoyed body attempted to roll to the right. Fireworks of pain shattered her temples, shot through her chest and left arm. Her stomach roiled as with the worst flu.

"Did she say something?" Anxiety darkened a woman's tone.

The bursts of agony did not diminish, but the familiar-sounding voice warmed Liz's heart. She searched her brain. What was the person's name?

"No, don't think so. She just moaned when she tried to move too fast."

A stranger. Liz attempted to open her eyes, but they refused to budge. Were they swollen shut? She lay immobile, but her questions would not be still. Where *was* she?

Someone spooned ice chips into her mouth. Cold, so cold, and she'd already been shivering. What kind of place was this? The ice froze her already uncooperative mouth. She couldn't tell them to stop. If she shook her heavy head, the excruciating fireworks might start all over again.

"Has the doctor said anything new?" A male voice spoke softly from a different direction. A pleasant, light fragrance of aftershave floated toward Liz. She'd smelled it before, hadn't she?

No identity floated through her mind, but her pulse beat a little faster. He sounded caring. Did he say something about a doctor? She must be in a hospital. How did she get here?

Her shoulder and ribs hurt worse than she thought possible. Was that an IV taped to her right hand? Moving was unbearable.

Listening seemed like too much work. Her inner murmurings faded into oblivion.

Liz awoke again. How much later, she had no idea. Were her eyes swollen shut as before?

Faint greenish light emanated from something nearby. Very slowly she turned her head. She could open her eyes a sliver, but she detected only fragments of digital numbers. A clock, she guessed. But even the smallest light hurt her eyes, and the nausea returned. She shut them again.

"If only we could get ahold of Miriam! But her brother said she went to see her sister in Ohio. She doesn't have a phone."

This woman sounded different from Liz's earlier visitors. "Sometimes her brother-in-law won't even receive a message."

Liz liked that straight-shooting voice. Something told her she liked Miriam too—whoever she was. But the name brought on a flood of anxiety.

"The doctor says Liz should be more like herself within a few days," a prim-voiced visitor said. "Otherwise, I'd run over there myself."

"You and me and Penelope," the straight shooter declared.

"Me on a motorcycle? No thank you." The prim woman laughed, but Liz heard steel in her tone. "I know you love that thing, but I worry about you." A gentle finger touched Liz's shoulder. "Motorcycles scared those horses when Liz stopped to help, remember?"

At the mention of horses, Liz's chest squeezed all the air from her lungs.

A third voice added, "Thank God that farmer stopped and helped Mattie control those horses, or they might have killed Liz."

Mattie? The name sent a wave of rage through Liz so blistering she wanted to throw off her covers.

The concerned voice belonged to a friend whose name started with the letter . . . N. The woman continued, "Apparently, Reuben seemed more anxious about his horses and buggy than he did about

Mattie." Her kind voice hardened. "You'd think with one daughter in jail, he'd cherish the other."

"That Reuben," sniffed Straight Shooter, "is a piece of work." She added a few other choice words.

"I'll drop by soon and make sure Mattie's all right," Prim Voice said. Liz didn't like Reuben. But Mattie blew her apart.

Yet these kind people liked Mattie.

Cold sweat dribbled down Liz's face. An ache, like a small volcano, erupted inside her head. *No*, she wanted to shout, *don't go see Mattie!*

Instead, she simply yelled. Yelled and yelled.

"What in the world?"

"Liz!" Hands pushed Liz back onto the soft pillow. "What's the matter, dear?"

More hands helped pin her down.

"Nightmares," a stranger said. "Not unusual after a bad accident, especially with a severe concussion." A quick prick stung Liz's arm. "Doc ordered this if she became agitated."

Fatigue alone sapped Liz's turmoil, but a fog wafted, then rolled through her. Later, when consciousness fluttered, fear curled around her like a viper. Why was she so afraid? Bad dreams? She couldn't remember. No, something was threatening her, a real danger. What was it? They didn't allow horses in the hospital . . .

Mattie wasn't here, was she?

She tried to ask, but her thoughts couldn't seem to connect with her mouth.

Was Mattie one of these "kind" women? Sometimes Liz lay for what seemed like hours, terror strangling her throat, pounding her head.

Two people played gin nearby. Liz still couldn't bear the light, but she heard snatches of movies. The stranger appeared to be a nurse, who made it her business to awaken Liz every time she managed a really sound sleep.

That was okay. The more Liz stayed awake, the better. These people seemed clueless. Didn't they know about Mattie?

But Mattie wouldn't assault her in broad daylight. Not in a hospital. Occasionally, her fear levels fell.

From what everyone said, Liz had suffered a concussion, a broken collarbone, and fractured ribs, with multiple bruises. Maybe she should be glad she couldn't open her eyes and look in a mirror.

Sleep again. Now the guy was here, holding her hand. The others did too, but despite calluses on his fingers, she liked his big hand best. Though the fear never went away, she felt safer.

Women showed up once more. But soon one told the others to go home. "You've all been up the better part of two days. I'll be on the floor all night anyway. I'll keep an eye on Liz."

Panic seized her. "No!" Liz's lips finally obeyed her mind. "No, don't go!"

"She talked!"

"Yay, Liz!"

"She's coming back!"

The flurry of happy voices slapped against her like hard raindrops.

"Hush." Mary Ann's voice. "I'll stay."

Mary Ann!

Despite her suffocating fear and the pain shooting through her head, Liz exulted. She'd remembered her friend's name. She'd said something the others understood. Maybe she'd remember other names too, names besides Mattie's.

That name tasted like a caustic acid. Rage stirred in her again. She fought her covers and stiffened, trying to sit up.

"It's all right." The no-nonsense voice calmed her. "No one will bother you. I'll check on you constantly. Mary Ann will come back tomorrow."

"We'll all come back," N—Naomi—reassured her.

Liz collapsed on her pillow, her brief spurt of energy depleted.

But she'd remembered two names. She hoped the others would return soon. And maybe she'd understand the hot terror that spiraled through her, searing her thoughts.

After a herd of footsteps exited, the no-nonsense friend poked and probed Liz. She must be a nurse too. A nurse on a bicycle . . .

Liz must have slept awhile, because the constant activity outside her room had quieted somewhat. Nighttime?

She opened one eye a slit. Then a larger slit. The blessed darkness of the room helped. She opened it almost all the way! Her eye adjusted to the darkness. As long as she didn't look at the lighted clock, she could peer at the neutral, mostly blank walls and dark window without setting off her stomach again.

Caitlyn. That was the nurse's name. They had ridden bikes together, along with a young man. Jason. For some reason, sadness wafted through her. But Liz was remembering!

Even the fear had dissipated somewhat. She was lying in an ordinary, rather stark hospital room, being cared for by Caitlyn. Amazing how seeing her environment and knowing her caregiver helped ease anxiety. Liz yawned. So sleepy. Blast, turning over was a risky operation. How long before she could do it without thinking?

She was just drifting off when, on cue, the door opened. Time for more poking and probing. Liz said proudly, "Hi, Caitlyn." Funny how greeting her friend by name seemed like such a big deal.

Caitlyn didn't answer. Perhaps they'd changed shifts, and Caitlyn had gone home. Maybe the new nurse was simply checking on her, and the prodding would wait until real morning. Quiet settled around her like a soft blanket. Before Liz allowed herself to sink into dozy twilight, she opened one eye halfway.

When had someone brought her robe? It hung on the door in bunchy folds.

Not a robe.

A figure crouched there.

Liz's traitor throat shut down her scream.

Caitlyn had placed the call button in her hand. Where was it? Her fingers slowly hunted through her sheets.

The small figure inched away from the door. A hat hid his face.

By the clock's light, she saw the dark line of a pen and a pad of paper on her bedside table. Not much of a weapon. But she could stab out an eye if the intruder attacked from her good side. With one hand still seeking the call button, she slipped her other hand between the bed rails and grasped the pen.

Closer. The figure edged closer. Liz heard a slight rattle that reminded her of a grocery store.

A plastic bag?

Liz forced her throat open to scream. "Ah!" she croaked.

The figure gave a childish chuckle.

A woman.

Mattie.

"Why?" Liz croaked. "Why?"

In a flash, she grabbed at Liz's good wrist.

Liz raised a knee to protect it. Another impotent scream.

Her assailant came at her with the plastic bag.

Liz stabbed at Mattie with the pen. Stab. Stab.

Swiss curses, but the bag went over Liz's head. Hands tightened it around her neck. Tighter.

Smooth, hellish plastic flapped, then gripped her cheeks, nose, and mouth.

Dear God, I need air.

Tighter.

Small hole? Liz sucked at it. Stabbed again.

A childish shriek of rage.

Yells. Blows. Furniture scraping.

A woman's hands, young and strong, gripped Liz's neck, squeezing, squeezing.

Liz dropped the pen. *Dear Jesus, help* . . .

The hands turned to claws that raked her neck.

But they let go.

Finally, stillness, except for a woman's gasps for breath. Liz froze as young hands touched her again.

But they were the kind, capable hands, examining, poking. "Oh, Liz, are you all right?"

Liz opened both eyes. Her rescuer, breathing hard, touched Liz's cheek. Even in the dark, Liz could see one eye swelling. "Okay now."

Caitlyn yanked an extension cord from the TV and bound the unconscious assailant's hands behind her. She called hospital security. Then she removed the hat.

At the sight of Mattie's soft, girlish face, Liz's nausea returned with a vengeance. She fell back on her pillow, trying not to gag. And weep.

The nurse was at Liz's side in a second, soothing, massaging, holding a glass of water with a straw to her lips.

When Liz had calmed herself, she said, "Caitlyn, how . . . ?"

Her defender smiled. "How did I learn kickboxing? Not part of the usual nursing curriculum. I learned when I was dating Mitch a year ago. You remember him?"

Liz couldn't recall exactly why Mattie wanted to kill her, but she remembered the big guy with the shaved head, Caitlyn's numero uno for a while.

Caitlyn laughed wickedly. "Nice to know ex-boyfriends are good for something."

22

"I wanted to organize a parade for your homecoming, but Mary Ann wouldn't let me." Sadie stuck out her lower lip, but her blue eyes twinkled. Liz, sitting in a wheelchair at the hospital entrance, grinned. "I appreciate the thought, but if you throw a parade for me, I'd rather not lead one sitting in this thing. I want to twirl a baton in front of a band!"

If she wasn't celebrating like her high school self, Liz was twirling that baton in her heart. The days away from her inn had seemed like months. She could hardly wait to run her fingers over the worn, satiny finish of the front door, luxuriate in front of her fireplace, and breathe in the woodsy fragrance that was home—so different from the medicinal smell that had greeted her nose every morning.

Caitlyn fussed over her. She'd insisted on the wheelchair, though Liz could walk fine for limited distances. "Every inpatient leaves this hospital in a wheelchair. No exceptions." She repeated Liz's dismissal instructions—again.

Liz retorted, "I may have lost my short-term memory for a few days, but I'm back, remember?"

The relief on both Caitlyn's and Sadie's faces amused her. Liz kept that mind-set, not wanting to think of her helplessness the first few days after Mattie's attempts to kill her.

Mary Ann pulled up in the Sew Welcome van. Liz had received compassionate care in the hospital, but one thought dominated her heart and soul: *Let me out of here!*

The trees were losing some of their autumn leaves, yet downtown looked beautiful, even in the weak sunshine. When Mary Ann approached the inn, Liz asked if they could pause in front and simply take it in.

The inn's cheerful red siding and intricate white trim, its wide porch and tall windows with stained glass transoms all called a welcome to Liz. She stroked the front door before Sadie opened it, then entered. Beans greeted her as if she held a peanut butter sandwich in each hand. "He missed you so much," Sadie cooed as Liz scratched the bulldog's ears. "I've had a time of it, getting him to eat."

Yeah, right. Liz doubted he'd lost much sleep over her absence either. Even now, Beans plopped on his rug, snoring before she left the rotunda.

She embraced Sarah, who pushed aside her reserve and hugged Liz back.

"Thanks so much for everything," Liz whispered. She'd heard her young maid had not only cleaned like a madwoman so Liz could return to a pristine inn but had come often and stayed late to help Mary Ann and Sadie manage daily details.

Opal came too. Her proper, dignified presence had proved such a comfort when Liz was struggling during the first days of her hospitalization. Even then, Sadie's attempt to win Opal over to motorcycles had given Liz a smile. But now, she realized the opposite-poles duo had been trying to jog her memory.

Miriam made her usual understated entrance, but Liz knew her cousin's loving presence, after returning from Ohio, had accelerated her healing. Despite the busyness of her own life, Miriam planned to stay with Liz several days.

The Material Girls were like her sisters, Liz mused. But family— family made all the difference.

Naomi bustled in, a huge smile on her pretty face.

Liz hugged her. "How'd you get away from the bakery?" Naomi rarely made it to coffee hour.

"I put a Closed sign on the door." Naomi laughed. "I think Pleasant Creek will survive an hour and a half without cupcakes."

"You won't lose customers." Mary Ann rearranged pillows and gestured for Liz to sit. "They're addicts."

"Your customers are addicts too," Naomi teased. "They'll tolerate your shorter hours today, but if you ever consider closing the shop again, a crowd will show up with protest signs."

The banter and laughter helped return Liz to the world she'd known before, but she found it hard to let the others bring her coffee as if she were a guest, not the innkeeper.

However, she didn't object when they trundled in an enormous apple pie on a cart. Liz stared; the gorgeous, golden-crusted pastry must have measured at least two feet across.

"You missed the big pie at the festival because you were stuck at the Kappel Apple Race," Mary Ann said, "so we did the next best thing."

The Material Girls had outdone themselves this time. Tart yet sweetened with exactly the right amount of sugar, nutmeg, and cinnamon, the buttery apple pie could have fulfilled the fantasies of Johnny Appleseed himself.

The front doorbell chimed. Liz peered out the window. Jackson and Chief Houghton.

"I hope you don't mind that I asked them." Mary Ann looked apologetic. "Maybe this is a little much for your first day home."

"Not at all." Liz's reserves already were dropping, but she wouldn't miss this for anything. She smoothed her hair, hoping she looked better than she had in the hospital.

She didn't expect this surge of self-consciousness when Jackson greeted her. His strong but gentle grasp had reassured her at the hospital. What had she said while semiconscious?

The warm gaze from his hazel eyes helped settle her jitters, though they did nothing to cure the happy butterflies in her stomach.

While they ate pie, Liz's friends kept the conversation light and newsy.

When she could eat no more, she set down her fork, took a coffee refill from Opal, and said firmly, "You've told me very few details. I want to hear everything."

The others exchanged glances.

"I knew you would." Houghton sighed and ate his last bite of pie. "What do you want to know first?"

"Whether my guesses were right. First, I assume Mattie followed me to Miriam's. That's how she knew where to stage her one-buggy accident."

"Originally, Mattie wouldn't admit anything," the chief said, "but as she realized how bad her legal situation looks, she confessed to most of the stuff she did, hoping to plea bargain. She told us she'd followed you several times to become familiar with your habits. She knew you were trouble from the start. That's why she tore up your sheets. To scare you off."

Liz didn't like to picture Mattie destroying her cherished antiques, but it explained why no one seemed to have noticed the vandalism. "An Amish girl hanging laundry on a clothesline? An everyday sight around here."

"She's smart. Managed to throw us off the track for a while—with lots of help from Cleveland himself." Houghton grimaced. "If he hadn't given so many of his 'friends' reason to kill him, we would have concentrated first on the halfway-point volunteers as suspects. Plus, using the horses to commit murder was a stroke of genius. They would have stomped you to a pulp if Jess Maynard hadn't driven by."

Liz remembered Jess, a tattooed chain-smoker whose farm featured his dilapidated trailer and weathered shack of a barn. Not the Caped-Crusader type. "I'll go see him first thing to thank him."

"Thank God he was there." Mary Ann squeezed her hand.

Sadie waved her forkful of pie. "But for Jess, we'd be eating this at your wake."

Thank you for that warm fuzzy. Liz shuddered, then pushed the thought aside to focus on what she really wanted to know. "Of course, Mattie tried to murder me because she thought I had her number. But why did she kill Trent? She must have hated him for lying and cheating on her sister, but that went on for years." She leveled a look at Houghton. "Maybe it was more her father's increasing abuse that pushed her to murder?"

The chief nodded. "Though he'd mistreated his family off and on before, Reuben became more violent after Rose dragged her family's name through the mud. Especially after his wife's death." His flinty expression softened momentarily before his eyes ignited. "Still, that's no excuse."

Sadie shook a fist. "Why didn't she think of killing her dad instead?"

"He's her father. That's especially important to the Amish. Kill an authority figure?" Jackson shook his head. "Unthinkable, even if he's an abuser."

"She'd already lost her mother," Naomi interposed. "Her dad ruled every moment of her day. Despite his cruelty, maybe she couldn't picture life without him."

"It was a horrible life. With the family's reputation in ruins, Mattie had no chance of marrying well and leaving Reuben behind." Liz ignored the shadow of past nausea trying to return. "Was there one factor that pushed Mattie over the edge? That made her spike those granola bars with peanut oil?" She glanced at Houghton. "Maybe Trent had cast his spell over Mattie too. Then left her in the dust."

"Good guess." The chief scowled. "Or bad, depending on your point of view."

Angry mutterings filled the sitting room.

Mary Ann's face reddened almost to purple. "I hate to say it, but that man certainly deserved what he got!"

Her reaction was so different from her usual charitable nature that everyone stared.

Questions flew to Liz's lips. "When did he carry on trysts with Mattie? Wouldn't Rose have caught on? And while Rose spoke of her supposed engagement to Trent, Mattie said nothing about one."

The chief smiled sadly. "I don't think there were any trysts. At last year's Harvest Festival, he evidently flirted with Mattie. Despite Rose's experience, Mattie swallowed his line, expecting him to pursue her this year." His face tightened. "She said, 'He didn't even remember me.'"

For the first time, a twinge of pity stirred in Liz. Maybe someday she could visit Mattie and tell her would-be murderer that she forgave her.

The chief continued, "Also, Mattie had some . . . call it 'encouragement' to get rid of Cleveland."

"Her accomplice egged her on," Liz guessed. "The creep who attacked Aunt Ruth and tried to poison Uncle Amos's horse."

At Houghton's impassive face, Sadie shook her finger. "It wasn't Big Berky!"

"Right. You and Liz confirmed his alibi." Houghton scored a point for them in the air.

Sadie sidetracked the discussion for a few minutes, describing their visit to the Texas Tenderloin and Tattoo and offering to demonstrate her favorite line dance.

Mary Ann vetoed her suggestion. "Later. I want to hear the end of the story."

"Tell us what you think, Liz. Was there someone else behind this?" Houghton urged.

Caitlyn shot him a look. "She may not feel like doing that right now."

With similar frowns from Jackson and Opal, the chief flinched a little. "Sorry."

"No, I want to talk about it," Liz protested. "When I first thought Rose might have killed Trent, I also realized Reuben was a major suspect. He certainly had a strong motive! When Rose confessed, I wondered, twisted as Reuben is, if he'd incited her to murder. Whether aware of Mattie's infatuation with Trent or not, her father might have pushed both daughters to kill the guy who had ruined their lives. And that either way, in order to protect himself—more than them—he attacked my Amish kin who were trying to help me."

"You know I thought the same," the chief said. "When I arrested

Rose, she clammed up. Mattie did too, at first. I wondered if they were hiding their dad's part in it."

"So Reuben Stoltzfus helped engineer that boy's death by pressuring his children to kill?" Opal's mild eyes flashed. "How could a father act like that?"

"He's an abuser and a terrible parent," Liz agreed, "but I've questioned whether Reuben was the instigator in all this. Miriam told me Reuben was in Shipshewana during the race. That scrambled my theory. I didn't have time to confirm if he actually went to Shipshewana. Later, when I got my brain back"—she grinned a little—"but had to stay in that hospital bed, I thought about it. If he was in Shipshewana, then Reuben wasn't at the halfway point to 'run the show,' to make sure that his scheme for revenge was carried out." Liz shook her head. "Abusers are controllers. He tried to monitor every detail of his daughters' lives. Why would he have been absent at such a critical point?"

Caitlyn's forehead puckered. "It doesn't make sense, does it?"

As the others murmured assent, Liz turned to the chief. "You confirmed Reuben's being in Shipshewana, didn't you?"

He nodded.

"Reuben had come home by the time Aunt Ruth was assaulted," Liz continued, "and he could have tried to silence her and Uncle Amos to protect Mattie. But playing the self-sacrificing hero didn't exactly fit his profile. No, I think someone else conceived this plan and dumped the dirty work on the Stoltzfus sisters, succeeding in getting rid of Trent Cleveland."

"You're right." The chief smiled. "I'm *sure* you don't have any idea who that someone is."

"Well, yes. Noah Troyer."

Unanimous stunned silence.

Houghton smiled again. "Yep. Arrested him just this morning."

"What?"

"You're kidding!"

"No way!"

A babble of disbelief crescendoed until Sadie whistled with her fingers. She roared, "Quiet down! You'll give Liz a headache!"

Thank you, Sadie. That makes me feel so much better.

Liz explained her reasoning. "I asked myself who else felt like Trent was a major threat to him and his family. The answer wasn't too hard. Noah had suffered through his son's first broken engagement because of Trent. With another engagement of Nathan's nearly trashed, his father had decided this English wedding wrecker had to be dealt with. Noah might have even feared Trent would try to date Amy after her marriage to Nathan, and that was intolerable in Noah's eyes."

Mary Ann's hand went to her mouth. "The Troyers and the Stoltzfuses are related."

"I'm afraid they are. Cousins." Jackson's grim expression reminded Liz that he and Noah were kin too and that Jackson was invited to Nathan's upcoming wedding.

Liz patted his arm, sad to see he was affected as well. "I'd seen interaction between the Troyers and Stoltzfuses at the festival, but I didn't realize the connection until I put two and two together."

"Noah always said Rose and Mattie were the little girls he never had." Mary Ann's eyes moistened, yet flames kindled in their depths, anger that spread to all the others in the room. "How *could* he?"

Liz sighed. Families could be so good. Or so bad. "Mattie told her big, strong second cousin, whom she trusted more than her own father, about Trent's toying with Rose. She might not have mentioned her own fury toward him. One way or another, Noah saw his chance."

Liz went on, "He and Mattie seemed two of a kind: impulsive, vengeful, and sneaky. Already mad about Trent's threat to his son Nathan's marriage, Noah became Mattie's ally." She turned to Houghton again. "Did Noah hatch the peanut oil/granola bar plot, or did they plan that together?"

"I don't know yet," the chief admitted. "Right now, they're trading accusations. Noah insists he had absolutely nothing to do with Mattie's schemes, and until the attack on Ruth, he seemed to have covered his tracks well, letting Rose and Mattie take all the blame. But we just got back the DNA report on the hairs we took from Ruth's clothing. They matched his. That opened the way for us to also match the footprints outside your windows to his shoes."

Houghton's lips curved in a mirthless smile. "When you're talking jail time, even family loyalties can reach a breaking point. Speaking of which, Mattie has charged Reuben with abuse. She's pressuring Rose into charging him too, but I don't know if she'll cooperate. Bottom line, Rose confirmed Reuben's abuse, so I arrested him too." He shook his head. "Rose will be released soon, but between this case and the festival, it's been a busy week at the jail. And an awful one for the Amish community."

Amid the horrified buzz his words generated, the doorbell rang again. Liz, wilted by the afternoon, hoped it was a UPS man.

But weariness dissipated when her visitor entered. "Kiera!"

Her teen gardener's green eyes sparkled. Already, the girl's joie de vivre lightened Liz's heart.

"Wow, you look way better than you did in the hospital," Kiera said. "You looked so awful that I hardly recognized you!"

"Uh, thank you." Kiera's characteristic bluntness made Liz grin. "Sorry I don't remember your coming to see me. I was pretty foggy."

The others, most of whom hadn't seen Kiera for a while either, welcomed her and the happy news she'd been accepted by Indiana State University next year.

"They say my chances are good to get a scholarship," Kiera told them, "but we'll see."

Her upbeat presence lifted the atmosphere to one of celebration again. But watching Kiera, whose difficult background had pushed her to excel, Liz couldn't help thinking of Rose, who was only a few years older. Her fantasy fiancé had been killed by her sister, and her abusive father and scheming cousin faced criminal charges as well. What kind of future was in store for Rose? She still bore the censure of having loved an English man. Would her estranged friends and remaining relatives come to her aid?

Later, when Sadie cleared out visitors and Liz rested in her quarters, she knew that when she'd regained some strength, she would pay Rose a visit.

23

"Töchter, are you sure we should come here alone?" Aunt Ruth regarded Jess Maynard's ramshackle trailer, surrounded by a yard full of rusty metal objects. Only an old tire turned flower bed of scraggly marigolds brightened the scene.

"Jess saved my life. I doubt he wants to harm us." Liz patted her arm, reminding herself that her aunt, though spunky, was still suffering the effects of Noah's attack. "Why don't you stay in the car? I'll be back in a few minutes, and we'll go see Rose."

"Oh no. He needs to see immediately that you are not alone."

Liz smothered a chuckle. Aunt Ruth, wearing her Kapp and long navy dress, hardly resembled a bodyguard. But as they carefully picked their way to the door, Liz appreciated her motherly presence.

A rap on the door summoned no one. After Liz tried again, Aunt Ruth, gladness in her voice, suggested they leave. They had just turned to go when someone wrenched the metal door open.

Liz's rescuer, scraggly as his marigolds, looked at them groggily.

"Jess, I'm Liz Eckardt. You saved my life."

He blinked, as if he didn't know what she was talking about. Then his unshaven face lit up. "Oh yeah. Them horses were crazy! I'm surprised you're standing here in one piece."

"I wouldn't be if you hadn't stopped to help." Liz held out her hand. "I wanted to thank you."

Jess paused, then took her hand in his callused one. His shy smile spread into a grin that made Liz forget their surroundings. "Anyone would have done it."

Not necessarily. But Jess, her knight in stained blue jeans and worn work shirt, had not hesitated.

Puzzlement wove through his expression. "The cops told me later that the Amish girl *wanted* her horses to stomp you into the ground." He shook his shaggy head. "Man, I never would have expected that. Not in a million years. Guess people can fool you sometimes."

"Yes, they can." Liz pressed an envelope into his hand. "Just a small token of my appreciation. Thank you so very much."

"*Dänke.*" Aunt Ruth grasped his other hand, tears in her voice. "You saved my Liz."

Jess's face reddened. Apparently, he'd endured all the gratitude he could tolerate, so Liz took her aunt's arm and they returned to the car.

As Liz drove away, Jess stood in the door, holding the unopened envelope. Its contents had strapped Liz's cash flow—medical costs were piling up, and she'd had to cancel guests while she recovered. But how could she do otherwise? God was good. Through Jess, he had given her more years in Pleasant Creek. As Liz motored along, basking in the sunshine and her aunt's chatter, she hoped to make him glad he had done so.

She wasn't sure, however, what she could do to help Rose. From all accounts, Reuben had managed his farm quite well, so Rose might not be in immediate financial need. But she was alone. Had anyone reached out to her in this terrible period of sadness?

Liz pulled into the gravel driveway, cheered to see laundry flapping on the clotheslines. At least Rose hadn't been hiding in bed all day, though truthfully, Liz wouldn't have blamed her if she had.

When the young woman answered their knock, the emptiness of her eyes reminded Liz of a vacant church building. Liz didn't know what to say.

Aunt Ruth did. "Rose, which would you rather do: Come and stay at my house or have me stay at yours?"

The palest of pinks touched Rose's white cheeks. She turned to Ruth as if the older woman's words had awakened her from a hundred years' sleep. "I would like to stay at your house."

Cooking had never been Liz's favorite part of her B&B business, but after slow weeks of home recuperation, she exulted as she fried and crumbled bacon and mixed eggs for the casseroles she planned to bake for her celebration brunch. The Material Girls, Aunt Ruth's family, Uncle Amos and family, and, of course, Jackson were invited.

Mary Ann and Aunt Ruth, bustling around her kitchen, took turns fussing at Liz for doing too much, but she blissfully ignored them. The doctors had released her. She was free!

Rose scooped balls of butter, saying little. Aunt Ruth had told Liz that Mattie had discouraged Rose from further visits to the jail. "Perhaps Rose's presence reminds Mattie of her cowardice when her sister was arrested. Rose misses her so! Maybe Mattie will relent after a few lonely months in jail."

Liz hoped so. Now she edged next to the young woman and whispered, "Does Aunt Ruth tell you what to do too?"

"Of course." The smallest of twinkles brightened Rose's solemn eyes. "But mostly, I like it."

Not surprising that the love-hungry girl enjoyed a little bossy mothering. Today, Liz would too. Then she would look forward to serving guests next weekend, using her own methods and schedule.

Well before the casseroles were done, Mary Ann gave Liz a slight push and said, "Take a little walk outside with Rose. We'll finish here before everyone comes."

An indignant protest sprang to her lips, but Mary Ann and Ruth gave her simultaneous winks.

What's up? Liz exchanged glances with Rose. No hints there. She shrugged. "Whatever. If you want to kick me out of my own kitchen, I guess I can handle that. As long as you also kick me out when it's time for cleanup."

"We can do that." Aunt Ruth nodded. "Now, shoo."

Grabbing jackets, the younger women left through the four-season room. Liz pointed at the glassy surface of the lake, surprisingly sunlit this mild November day. "May as well enjoy it while we can."

Rose hesitated. "I . . . do believe Mrs. Berne and your aunt want you to see the parking lot."

"The parking lot?" *Okay.*

They changed direction and trudged toward the garage.

Liz halted in her tracks.

Unicycles. Decorated with streamers.

Kandy, Stephanie, and Jessi, plus Caitlyn and Jackson rode in a row across her parking lot under a large banner that read, We Love Liz! Surrounding the lot, half the town cheered.

Liz gasped.

A grinning Kandy sped effortlessly to the front. Reaching Liz, she hopped from her unicycle and hugged her. The others followed suit, including Jackson, who nearly tumbled but managed to recover.

He clasped her longer than her other friends did, then summoned his official voice. "As mayor of Pleasant Creek, I join the rest of our community in expressing our appreciation for your continual service. Not only has your business's reputation enhanced our town, but you have shown fearless dedication in maintaining justice and keeping it a safe place. For this, we thank you."

Whoops and applause greeted his speech.

Tears welled in her eyes at this wonderful but slightly bizarre tribute. They dribbled down her cheeks when she opened the envelope Jackson handed her. Her unbelieving eyes took in a large check for much more money than she'd given Jess.

Jackson waved a hand at the crowd. "Just a gift from a grateful town."

He then awarded Liz a baton. When her jaw dropped, he nudged her. "Well, you said you wanted to twirl a baton in front of a band, right? Come and lead your parade! On the back of Berky's motorcycle, of course."

The big man emerged from the crowd on his rumbling Harley and bowed like a Shakespearean actor. "Your ride, ma'am."

Liz finally found her voice. Sort of. "Th-thank you all." She started to insist on walking, but seeing his practiced courtliness, dipped in a small curtsy. "I am honored."

He and the other bikers—minus Honey—with a resplendent Sadie and Beans, fired up their motorcycles. Liz donned the helmet Shine handed her and mounted Big Berky's bike behind him. With a roar, they pulled onto Main Street, followed by the small but mighty local high school band and the unicyclists. Kandy, agile as a circus performer, astonished the crowd with her tricks.

Holding on to Big Berky's huge frame with one arm was challenge enough. Twirling the baton with the other hand without clobbering them both proved an even bigger one. But she did it, adding a few variations as they wound around the town square.

At the end, when Liz dismounted, she tossed the baton into the air, high as her heart's joy, and caught it. *Ta-da!*

Her onlookers yelled and applauded. Jackson's face glowed.

Of course, Mary Ann and the other Material Girls, with Aunt Ruth's help, had planned for the celebratory horde. While she was leading her own parade, a crew from Liz's church set up tables and chairs in every corner of the inn and backyard. Sneaky Naomi had baked extra casseroles in her big ovens, and each family who came brought a dish to share—breakfast meats, casseroles, quiches, breads, and fruit. With festival food such a recent memory, Liz marveled that anyone could consume such a banquet.

But Pleasant Creek never backed down from this sort of challenge.

Liz also feasted on the townspeople's kind concern and assurance of their continued prayers for her strength and healing.

"And for your safety," one old gentleman said as he shook her hand. "The bad guys just seem to flock to you, don't they?"

But the good guys did too. Through the tragedy of Trent's death, her recent guests had become close friends. Eating with them in the four-season room, Liz heard Kandy's good news that she'd won another major race.

"The national association is beginning to take a look at Kandy," Stephanie bragged.

"About time," Jessi concurred. "She's on her way to the top."

"I'm taking you guys with me." Kandy broke an extra-large cheese Danish into three pieces and shared them with her cycling buddies.

How different from Trent and Jason.

Jason. Liz couldn't bear to ask about him.

Kandy seemed to understand how much Liz needed to know. He was still out on bail but could not leave his hometown. "Jason's trial is coming up in a month, but his lawyer seems to think that given his clean record, he should draw a light sentence, perhaps house arrest instead of jail." Her smile appeared forced. "He helps out at bike meetings and rides. Even if he doesn't receive a prison term, he won't be able to race for a long time. Maybe never."

"I'm sure Jason has you girls to thank for keeping him in the loop." Liz squeezed Kandy's hand.

"Caitlyn has helped too." Kandy glanced at their friend, talking to Jessi and Stephanie. "She's come to see him a couple of times."

Caitlyn hadn't said a word about Jason. Liz also resolved to say nothing, even to the other Material Girls. Caitlyn would talk about Jason if and when she was ready.

The surprise party broke up earlier than most community events, probably because Mary Ann had cautioned everyone to remember Liz's recent hospitalization. After pitching in to clean up, the townspeople went home.

Jackson lingered, helping to wash dishes until Mary Ann chased him and Liz from the kitchen.

"Want to sit in the backyard?" Liz hated to waste such mild weather by staying inside.

"Sounds like a plan." He followed her to her bench. "A little rest won't hurt you at all."

A little quiet would be nice too. She leaned back, inhaling the brisk air, admiring patches of gold and scarlet here and there that contrasted with bare, black trees and cerulean sky.

They sat awhile in comfortable silence.

Finally, Jackson said, "The last time we talked here, I told you the cycling association had threatened to disown us. Things are better now that the media's found new subjects to hound."

"The association's agreed to keep sanctioning the Kappel Apple Race?"

"We're talking. And making progress." He shot her one of his boyish grins. "It's a good thing the mayor is such a diplomatic guy."

"Humble too." Liz rolled her eyes.

"Humble," he agreed, "and a lousy unicyclist."

She laughed. "How long have you been riding that thing?"

"Only a couple of weeks, after Kandy first came up with this idea for your party."

"You must have practiced a lot." Other than his dismount, Jackson had ridden surprisingly well.

"I did." He leaned toward her. "I thought if I impressed you on the unicycle, then maybe you . . ."

Maybe I might try unicycling? She shifted. "Um, I don't think Doc would agree to my doing something like that for a while."

"Oh no. Not now. And not unicycling." His words tripped over each other.

"What do you mean?"

A slight flush colored his face. "If you saw I had mastered the unicycle, you might trust me enough to ride a tandem at next year's Kappel Apple Ride." Jackson added quickly, "If the doc says it's all right." He sounded like a teen—minus the squeaky voice. Endearing.

"Perhaps we might try again next spring." She looked at him

from under her lashes. "Because I do trust you, Jackson. Unicycle or no unicycle."

His eyes had widened. He moved closer.

She lifted her chin. "We will, however, have to have an extended discussion about dogs."

"Dogs? Oh yeah. Dogs," Jackson mumbled, then leaned back and put his arm around her shoulders.

Even as she snuggled into his friendly embrace, her always active mind questioned: Would they ever pedal in rhythm together?

Who knew?

But she sure wouldn't mind trying.

Learn more about Annie's fiction books at

AnniesFiction.com

- Access your e-books
- Discover exciting new series
- Read sample chapters
- Watch video book trailers
- Share your feedback

We've designed the Annie's Fiction website especially for you!

Plus, manage your account online!

- Check your account status
- Make payments online
- Update your address

Visit us at AnniesFiction.com